Muskie Attack
An Up North Adventure

Muskie Attack
An Up North Adventure

G.M. Moore

Muskie Attack: An Up North Adventure

ISBN: 978-1475004298

Printed in the United States of America

For my father, James Moore

If you would only write a book …

Lost Land Lake

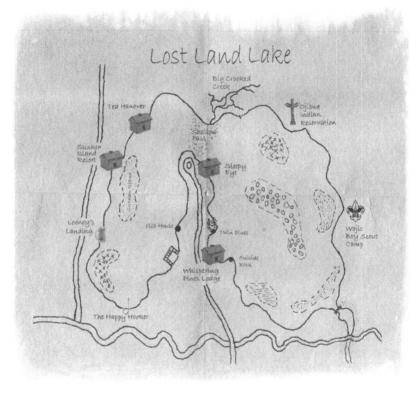

WAY UP NORTH

Corbett Griffith III was turning a slight shade of green. He took in a deep breath, puffed his cheeks out, and let out a burst of air. He inhaled and exhaled, inhaled and exhaled—all in an attempt to keep the lunch he had eaten an hour earlier down. The SUV he was seated in continued its roller coaster of a ride through the North Woods of Wisconsin: curve to the right, curve to the left, up a hill, down a hill.

This isn't going to work, he thought, still puffing air in and out. *I'm going to throw up all over the backseat of this car. Great way to start the summer.*

Great way, indeed. Corbett didn't even want to be here. Definitely not in Wisconsin, state of the cheese head. Definitely not on this vomit-inducing road. And definitely not in the backseat of this SUV bearing the bumper sticker, "Fight Crime. Shoot Back. Jim's Gun Shop. Minong, Wis." If given the choice, which he wasn't, he would have spent his break playing video

1

games, working on his computer, or taking fossil and archaeology classes at Chicago's Field Museum.

"How's it going back there?" his uncle asked from the front seat. Then he chuckled. "You don't look so good."

"Not feeling so good," Corbett replied.

"Not to worry. We're almost there."

There was Uncle Dell's Whispering Pines Lodge, a fishing resort and the place Corbett would be spending the months of July and August.

Since his parents' divorce more than a year ago, Corbett's mother had become increasingly worried about him. She wanted his father, a Chicago businessman, to spend more time with Corbett: take him canoeing, fishing, and swimming. "A ten-year-old boy should be out having adventures, not reading about them," she would say.

But to Corbett's dad, Corbett Griffith II, an outdoor adventure meant a trip to the putting green. Corbett longed to spend more time with his father. He would do anything to get his attention, including putting, which Corbett thought was boring. But he was never asked. His mother was actually no better. An editor at the *Chicago Sun-Times*, she had deadlines and late-breaking stories that kept her away from home—a lot. So ... enter Uncle Dell.

Corbett overheard the phone conversation his mother had had with her much older brother in early June. He had been quietly listening at the head of the stairs.

"He's getting pudgy, Dell. I can't have him trapped inside for another summer. It's as if he's afraid of the outdoors. He yells if a bug comes near him. He won't even pet a dog. I don't understand it. He needs to get outside and be a boy."

Be a boy! Corbett thought incredulously, remembering the conversation. *Who am I? Pinocchio?* Maybe he was slightly pudgy, and, OK, maybe he was a little afraid (bugs did creep him out, and dogs scared him, especially the big barking ones), but was that really a good reason to send him away? Apparently it was, because as soon as school let out for summer break, Corbett found himself shopping and packing for a two-month stay in Wisconsin. He would be, his mother announced, helping Uncle Dell at Whispering Pines Lodge. Uncle Dell had a difficult time finding reliable help, and Corbett needed an adventure in the great outdoors.

This is definitely the great outdoors, Corbett thought, looking out the car window. He could see nothing but woods on either side of the road. The occasional mailbox popped out of the underbrush indicating that a home was in there somewhere, but Corbett couldn't see any. All he could see was a blur of white pine, hemlock, and yellow birch trees as they raced down County A. Since leaving the Village of Minong, he and Uncle Dell had passed only two other vehicles, both towing boats behind them.

Whispering Pines Lodge was perfect, his mother had said. Corbett would have work to do, but also plenty of free time to explore. *Yeah, it's perfect*, Corbett thought, still staring out the car window, but not for him. It was perfect for his parents. Corbett knew his parents loved him, but he also knew that *their* lives came first, not his. They had no time for him. He thought of himself as a check mark on their to-do lists.

Career, check.

Marriage, check.

City condo, check.

Child, check.

Divorce, check.

Ship child off, check.

Corbett sighed heavily, resigning himself to his fate. The afternoon sun streamed into the car. *Well, Wisconsin is kind of pretty—and peaceful*, he reluctantly admitted.

"Pay attention now, Corbett," Uncle Dell commanded from the front seat. "We're coming to the first fork."

Looming ahead, Corbett saw, was a fork in the road, and in the middle of that fork had to be about fifty signs, all shaped like arrows, all white with black letters, all attached to the same two poles. Most of the signs had people's names on them; all had mileage: Tomasik one mile, Snider five miles, Moore two miles.

"You see Whispering Pines, four miles? Ninth one down on the left? That's us. We stay left. Easier to remember left than try to find the sign."

Corbett nodded. He was starting to cheer up and feel a little better. He cracked the car window and got a good whiff of fresh air. *Ahhhhhhhhh much better*, he sighed.

The trip had been a long one—about seven hours stuck in a car. His mother had driven him from Chicago to Madison, Wisconsin, where Uncle Dell had picked him up for the journey much farther north. It was closing in on two o'clock in the afternoon, and Corbett was ready to be there. And there, as far as he was concerned just then, could be anywhere.

"Fork number two approaching," Uncle Dell called out. This time the sign was on the right and said two miles.

Getting there, getting there, finally getting there, Corbett chanted in his mind. And surprisingly, he found himself excited and eager to see exactly where "there" was.

"It gets a little trickier from here," Uncle Dell explained as the SUV took the right fork. "The sign for Peninsula Road—our road—is hard to see. Get a lot of complaints from guests about that. They get lost all the time. But we're in the middle of the Chequamegon National Forest, and the DNR ..." Uncle Dell paused and looked at Corbett in the rearview mirror. "That's the Department of Natural Resources."

Corbett nodded even though he had no idea what the DNR or the Department of Natural Resources was.

"OK. Anyway, they've got rules and regulations. So does the county for that matter. Look on the right side of the road. We'll pass a culvert, and then about a fourth mile up is the sign. It's about waist high, surrounded by Wild Columbine."

Corbett sat up straighter and looked.

And looked.

And looked.

The winding, hilly road made the distance seem much, much longer.

"Culvert," Uncle Dell called, pointing to the right. And there, poking out from under the road and into a swamplike area was a large metal cylinder. *Now for the sign*, Corbett thought, looking at the road ahead more intently. But Corbett never saw a sign. Before he knew what had happened, the SUV took a turn into the woods.

The sun vanished. The paved road disappeared. The trees grew closer. Corbett gulped and his blue eyes widened. *Lions and tigers and bears. Oh my.* The line from *The Wizard of Oz* echoed through his mind. Still peering out the window, he clutched the top of the passenger door. *Where, oh where, are we going?* his panicked mind wondered.

The SUV was now making its way down a narrow road that was "paved" with a mixture of sand, soil, and rock. Numerous potholes kept the car and its passengers rocking up and down and back and forth. Tree branches continually scraped the sides of the car. The SUV splashed into a particularly large pothole that propelled Uncle Dell so far off his seat that his head hit the car's roof.

Uncle Dell rubbed the top of his crew-cut head, then shook it in disgust.

"The county is supposed to be fixing all this," he complained. "I've called, and I've called."

Deeper and deeper into the woods they went. Corbett noticed the SUV's thermometer, which had read seventy-two in town, had dropped to sixty-six. *This is not good*, he thought. Corbett now understood why Link Bros. Grocery in Minong offered everything in bulk. Corbett had marveled at the gallon-sized jars of mustard, relish, and ketchup when he and Uncle Dell had shopped there before heading to the lodge. There was definitely no 7-Eleven to grab a quick slushy at out here.

Just then, movement on the road ahead caught Corbett's attention.

"It's a deer!" he shouted, as the animal bolted off the road and into the woods.

Uncle Dell slowed the car.

"Look, there're two others," he said, pointing to a spot just off the road.

One minute the deer were there, and then with a flick of the tail and a leap, they were gone.

"Wow. Cool," Corbett gushed. "I've only seen deer at the Brookfield petting zoo."

"You'll see plenty more," Uncle Dell said. "And maybe a bear or two."

"Bears?" Corbett asked, his mouth feeling suddenly dry. "Really? There are bears?"

"Yep. Ornery things, too. Kinda look like big black dogs, at first. You'll see."

The SUV had bumped its way about a mile into the woods when it crossed over another culvert that led into a small pond filled with lily pads and cattails. Corbett noticed something sticking up out of the water but couldn't quite make out what it was. It looked like the back of a very large turtle, a tortoise perhaps. *But that is impossible*, Corbett thought. *Tortoises don't live in the wild of Wisconsin.* He quickly forgot about the large mound as the SUV took a turn that revealed a road spotted with mailboxes and carved signs telling them they were passing Heffner's Hideaway or Richardson's Retreat.

Finally, the woods drew farther and farther back. Patches of grass, sand, and pine needles covered the ground. They were now driving on a peninsula, a narrow strip of land that jutted out into the lake. The bright afternoon sun, which had been hidden moments before, sparkled like diamonds on the water surrounding them. Uncle Dell stopped the SUV in front of two behemoth black bears. He smiled, pointed to the sign the carved bears held high, and said, "Welcome to Whispering Pines."

Uncle Dell unloaded Corbett's bags, tossing them quickly onto the lodge's screened porch. Its door banged shut loudly behind him, causing an already skittish Corbett to jump. Uncle Dell smiled reassuringly and placed a hand on Corbett's shoulder.

7

"Not to worry, now," he said. "You're going to like it here. No question. Come on. Let's check the place out."

Corbett smiled back politely and began to walk with Uncle Dell among the cabins and outbuildings that dotted the small peninsula where Whispering Pines made its home. The waters of Lost Land Lake surrounded the mile-long strip of land, which was only an eighth mile across at its widest. The peninsula slowly narrowed to a point that ended in a part of the lake known as Shallow Pass.

Uncle Dell reminisced while the two walked, explaining that Whispering Pines Lodge was built in the mid-1940s—back in the days of master fisherman and world record holder Louis Spray.

"You've heard of the good ol' days?" Uncle Dell asked.

Corbett nodded that he had.

"Well, that was them all right. Eleven-pound bass and thirty-eight-pound northern pike ruled the lakes. Game fishing was at its peak."

Uncle Dell paused, as if waiting for a reaction. Corbett guessed he was supposed to be impressed by this, but he wasn't sure. He didn't know what game fishing was.

"Wow," he finally responded.

Uncle Dell seemed pleased and continued on. "Our guests don't require a lot of pampering," Dell explained. "Peace and quiet. That's all they need. The lodge holds the only phone and television on the place. The guest phone is for emergencies only. Remember that," he instructed.

Corbett nodded OK.

"And the TV gets very poor reception—no cable, no satellite hookup here."

Corbett nodded OK again.

"And no cell phones," Dell continued. "They don't work out here. Can't get the Internet, either."

Corbett stared at his uncle in disbelief. *This is just like Gilligan's Island,* he thought, remembering the old TV show he often watched by himself after school. He sang the theme song in his head: *No phones, no lights, no motor cars. Not a single luxury.*

"The radio is always an option," Uncle Dell was saying, "but the only station that comes in clearly is one out of Rice Lake. It plays oldies country—a lot of Hank Williams, a lot of Johnny Horton."

Corbett was in a slight daze. He slowly nodded OK yet again. Did Uncle Dell really think he would like it here? Was he nuts? His mom promised a summer of fun. A summer of boredom was more like it. What was he supposed to do without TV or the Internet?

"Here we go," Dell said stopping in front of Cabin 3. "The Coopersmiths haven't arrived yet. Come on in and have a look around."

Corbett and Uncle Dell entered one of Whispering Pines' twelve brown, clapboard cabins. The rustic cabin featured a kitchen, three bedrooms, a bathroom, and a screened porch. The bathroom held only a toilet. Corbett thought it looked as if someone took an outhouse and simply attached it to the side of the cabin.

"The cabins still have many of their original furnishings," Uncle Dell bragged as he showed Corbett beds with metal head- and footboards, a table with chrome legs and a hard plasticlike surface, log chairs, and antique dressers and mirrors.

"If you really want to step back in time, poke around the kitchen a bit while I go get my tools. This hinge needs fixing," Uncle Dell said as he rattled the bathroom door.

Stepping into a Whispering Pines kitchen, Corbett discovered, was like stepping into a bygone era. The old-fashioned refrigerator had a small upper freezer that, when opened, looked like a cave of ice. The gas stove only lit with matches. The cabinets were filled with items long since replaced in modern kitchens. Corbett found a mixer that required hand power to turn its beaters, a toaster with doors instead of slots that required the bread to be rotated by hand, and a cordless coffeepot that had a strange bubblelike knob on top.

When Uncle Dell returned, he had a man with him. "Corbett, this here is Mr. Hugh Goodner. He's in Cabin 5."

"So here's the young man himself!" Hugh greeted Corbett happily with a handshake. "Dell's in need of a few good hands. My wife won't let me unload one item from the car until she gives the cabin a good cleaning herself. Isn't that right, Dell?"

"Yes, that's right," Dell answered. He rolled his eyes as he walked by so only Corbett could see.

Dell went to work on the bathroom door as Hugh pulled Corbett aside. His hair was greased back, and he smelled of fish and bad aftershave. Corbett didn't want to get too close, but Hugh drew him in tight.

He led Corbett first to a window. "See," he pointed.

Dead flies and spiders filled the windowsill.

Next, Hugh led him to the front door. "See."

Sand and cobwebs coated the door screen.

Hugh took him to a corner of the kitchen. "See there."

Dirt and dust clogged the corner.

"Yuck," Corbett muttered. He really wished he'd packed hand sanitizer. He was afraid to touch anything now. Who knew what germs were growing in here?

"It's OK," Hugh whispered. "We're all used to it. Part of the place's charm, ya know." He winked at Corbett conspiratorially. Then he spoke louder. "Good help is hard to find. That right, Dell?"

"Yep. Good help and good wives."

"So they are. So they are," Hugh chuckled. "Don't go tellin' Vera I said that now, but I know you've had your share of wife woes, Dell."

Uncle Dell reentered the kitchen. The door was now fixed.

Corbett looked at him perplexed. "I had an aunt?" he asked. He had never heard of an aunt before. He didn't think really old people got divorced. "Did she die?"

"Well, actually you had three aunts. And, no, none of them died. Let's just say life Up North can be rough."

"Yeah, I know. There's no TV," Corbett replied.

Dell and Hugh laughed heartedly at that.

"No, no. Not because there's no TV. Well, at least I don't think it was because of the TV," Dell chuckled and tousled Corbett's dark brown hair.

As they walked back to the lodge with Hugh still in tow, Uncle Dell told Corbett exactly what happened to each of his wives.

Wife number one left after her second winter. So much snow fell that the Everses couldn't see out of the lodge's windows or open the front door for weeks at a time. Peninsula Road, along with others in the area, became narrow tunnels of snow. Residents attached six-foot-high bicycle flags to their cars in order to see oncoming traffic. That season the Minong area recorded about two hundred inches of snow—more than enough for wife number one to head south.

Wife number two fell victim to a friendly fly infestation the summer of her fifth year at Whispering Pines. Dell explained that the flies were just part of nature's cycle, sent to control a growing population of caterpillars. The insects were eating away at the surrounding foliage, and it was nature's way of stopping them. That cycle occurred every ten years or so. It was no big deal. The flies wouldn't bite, but they did have a nasty habit of regurgitating where they landed. Hundreds of vomiting flies covering her from head to toe were enough to send wife number two packing.

Uncle Dell learned a little with wife number three. He took her to Florida for the winter, and with the friendly flies still dormant, he didn't foresee a problem there. However, he also didn't foresee wife number three's intolerance to insect bites. The summer months of June and July proved to be her undoing. Deer flies, stable flies, no-see-ums, mosquitoes, and other bloodsucking arthropods kept her body covered in itchy red welts that never seemed to go away. She incessantly sprayed herself with insect repellent. It was no help. She covered herself from head to toe with netting. No help. She finally refused to step foot outside. Still, no help. When her bite-riddled ears swelled to the size of red peppers, she could stand no more and hightailed it out of the North Woods.

"And I've been happily single ever since," Dell concluded. "Wisconsin is all I need. The cool, damp mornings; the sun not fully setting until after 9:00 PM; the clean, star-speckled night sky."

"What about winter?" Hugh asked. "You still up here all winter?"

"Oh, no," Dell replied. "I spend winters in Florida."

It was now dusk, and Dell was getting Corbett settled in at the lodge. He took Corbett through the kitchen to a small hallway where Corbett's suitcases and gear were stacked. The hallway had three doors leading off it. To the right was Uncle Dell's office, to the left a spare bedroom, and straight ahead a bathroom. Corbett picked up one of his bags and started to carry it into the spare room.

"Hold up," Uncle Dell said and grabbed Corbett by the shoulder. "That's not where you're sleeping." He took a few steps down the hall, stopped in front of the bathroom door, and pointed up. "I thought the loft might suit you better."

Corbett hadn't noticed the ladder running up the wall right next to the bathroom door. Looking up, he saw a square hole cut in the ceiling.

"Go on up. Check it out," Uncle Dell coaxed. "There's a light switch down here and one up there."

So Corbett flicked on the light and started slowly, slowly up the ladder, one rung at a time.

"Wait," Uncle Dell called out, throwing a bag over Corbett's shoulder. "Take something with you. Once you get up, I'll pass the rest of your gear."

Corbett climbed up just enough to poke his head through the square opening. He quickly looked around like a gopher just popping out of its hole.

"Cool," Corbett said as he finally hoisted himself up into the room. *Now this I'm going to like.*

The small room held only a bed, a chair, and a table—all made from birch tree logs. Two large, screened windows filled opposing walls and offered views of Lost Land Lake's Whispering Pines Bay on one side and of the woods on the other. What Corbett found the most interesting about the room was the array of mounted fish and old lures that decorated the walls and peaked ceiling. Corbett would sleep every night with a four-and-a-half-pound walleye over his head.

A loud thud caught Corbett's attention, and he turned to see that one of his bags had just been flung into the room. Corbett ran over to the ladder to help Uncle Dell get the remaining bags up.

"What do you think?" Dell asked.

Corbett grinned. "It's awesome, Uncle Dell."

"Good, good," Dell said. "Now get settled in up here and get to bed. There's work to be done tomorrow, starting with filling in some of those potholes." He headed down the ladder, then stopped and yelled up, "You can meet Pike tomorrow. It's going to take the two of you, I think."

Corbett leaned over the hole in the floor to ask, "Who's Pike?"

"Tomorrow," Uncle Dell said. "You'll find out tomorrow."

OUT ON THE LAKE

An eerie film of fog covered the bay outside Corbett's loft window. The day was beginning in typical fashion for northern Wisconsin: overcast and drizzling rain. Not many fishermen braved the waters this early morning. Lost Land Lake sat quiet except for a few distant boats. A family of ducks meandered its way along the bay's shore. The mother and eight ducklings paddled along in a row, swimming around or under the docks that poked out from the shore and into the lake. The ducklings occasionally broke order to dive for food. Heads dipped down. Tails shot up. Frantic ducklings would then race to catch up with the rest of the family. A school of baby catfish caught one duckling's attention, and a chase ensued. The young duck playfully paddled after the fish; he dove and missed, dove and missed, paddled farther out, dove and missed, and then dove and missed. Finally, noticing his family had reached and was about to pass the next dock, the duckling left the school behind.

Paddling fast, the little duck tried to catch up to his family, but a quick tug on his webbed feet stopped him short. Then, a second more forceful tug pulled the little duck under water. He bobbed back up, squawking as loud as his lungs would allow. Up the shoreline, his mother turned at the sound and squawked loudly back. The duckling frantically flapped its small wings, fighting to stay above water, but the pull beneath was too strong. The duckling went under and vanished.

A fearful quiet filled the bay as the water's surface rippled with movement. The mother duck, sensing danger, scurried her family out of the water and on to the shore.

A long, rust-colored fin broke the water's surface for a moment—and then was gone.

MEET PIKE

It was late morning, and Corbett was up in the loft unpacking his suitcases. He found that the birch table doubled as a dresser with shelving hidden behind a fabric skirt. A mirrored medicine cabinet where he put items such as his toothbrush and comb hung just to the left of the loft's ladder. He had opened the windows, and a nice breeze blew through the room, billowing out the curtains.

"Hey! You! ... Up there!" came a yell from outside. "Hey! Come on!"

Corbett went to the window and looked down to see a tall, athletic-looking boy standing impatiently with his arms crossed. He was wearing a bright yellow and orange tie-dyed T-shirt with a decal of a flying eagle emblazoned across the front and camouflage shorts that hit just below his knee. Tied on his head was a black bandana decorated with skulls and crossbones. Tufts of sandy blond hair stuck out from underneath it. Corbett looked down at his dark blue polo shirt and khaki shorts. He definitely didn't fit in Up North. And he definitely didn't want to go anywhere with this boy he figured had to be Pike.

Uncle Dell told Corbett all about Pike over breakfast. Although it was obvious Uncle Dell thought highly of Pike, it also was obvious to Corbett that his own thoughts had been right: this boy was trouble. Plus, the two of them had nothing in common.

$$* \quad * \quad * \quad *$$

Unlike Corbett, indoors was not the place eleven-year-old Pike McKendrick wanted to be. He'd grown up fishing, hunting, and camping around the lakes of northern Wisconsin. Uncle Dell said he had the spirit of an adventurer, which tended to get him into trouble—a lot.

"That boy went in search of a tributary stream off Lost Land Lake a week or so ago," Uncle Dell recalled with admiration. "He discovered it on an old map of the lake and had to investigate. It turned out not to be much of a stream. It was more of a shallow, winding bog."

While navigating a kayak through the tangles of fallen trees, grasses, and wild irises, the story went, Pike had spotted a frog. Very froglike himself, he'd leaped from the kayak to pursue the small creature. Very unfroglike, his feet had gotten mired in the muck. He'd sunk calf-deep before his grandpa, who had accompanied him on the outing, was able to pull him out. Pike made it safely back to his kayak, but one of his shoes did not. It was sucked off his foot by the soggy black goo.

"Was his mother mad!" Uncle Dell exclaimed with a chuckle. "She sent Pike and his grandpa back to retrieve it, but even the claws of a pitchfork couldn't dislodge the missing shoe. Or maybe they were in the wrong spot?" Dell shrugged. "The bends and curves of a bog all begin to look alike after a while. The shoe is still somewhere at the bottom of that so-called stream."

This seemed to be a typical adventure for Pike and for those having the misfortune of accompanying him, Corbett feared.

"Pike's got a way of getting people—except his mother, of course—to do things," Uncle Dell explained. "An exasperated sigh, a roll of the eyes, and an impatient 'Come on. Just do it' usually does the trick."

Pike's family owned The Happy Hooker, a bait, tackle, and convenience store located on the banks of Lost Land Lake. Fishermen would boat over or drive in off County A for supplies or the latest fishing news.

"It's a real family business—everyone pitches in," Uncle Dell said.

"So why does Pike work here and not at The Happy Hooker?" Corbett asked.

"Let's just say Whispering Pines suits Pike a little better," Uncle Dell chuckled and told Corbett why.

Running The Happy Hooker was supposed to be a family affair with Pike and his older sister, Gil, becoming employees as soon as school let out. Gil took to operating the cash register, processing fishing licenses, and taking grocery orders right away. Pike, on the other hand, did not take to any of these tasks. He was easily distracted. Plus, he complained incessantly about being bored. So, his parents moved him off the front desk and over to bait, which they thought would suit him better. And it did. The problem was, it didn't suit many of the customers.

"Folks never knew what they would run into back in The Happy Hooker bait room." Uncle Dell shook his head in amusement at the thought. "Whatever Pike caught and wanted to keep—turtles, frogs, snakes, suckerfish, you name it—ended up in the bait room or in its tanks. You should have heard the yelps, cries, and screams from customers."

Corbett grimaced. He was sure he would have been one of the yelpers.

Pike, it seemed, also couldn't keep his hands off the bait. He constantly played with the minnows, leeches, grubs, and worms. He thought nothing of carrying an assortment of live bait around and showing it off to squeamish vacationers. The end of Pike's Happy Hooker career came when a banker from Duluth left the store with an escaped leech firmly attached to his sandal-clad foot.

"The commotion and hysteria that man generated." Dell snorted his contempt. "Well, that was it for Pike. So, like your mom, the McKendricks asked me to take on Pike here. They couldn't have him go unsupervised all summer, and I need the help."

This was Pike's third summer helping out at Whispering Pines, and from what Dell said, both thought they were getting the better end of the deal. For a weekly allowance, Pike cleaned the fish house, raked up the swimming area, helped with garbage collection, mowed the grass, mopped off the docks, and did any other chore Dell could come up with.

"For Pike, I think it's like summer camp," Uncle Dell explained. "The chores really don't take that long, and then he can fish, swim, and explore the woods all he wants. He likes hanging out with the guests, too. There's always someone to go fishing with around here. What's not to like?"

Corbett grimaced again. He could think of a few things.

$$* \quad * \quad * \quad *$$

"Hurry up!" Pike yelled. He was waving at Corbett to come down. "Dell is letting us take the cart!"

Corbett looked around until he spied what used to be a golf cart. It now looked like a mini-jeep, beat-up and painted army green. The teenage workers at Whispering Pines had left their mark on the cart over the years, covering it with bumper stickers and decals from across the country and around the world. One sticker was never touched by another or covered in any way. It stretched across the hood and read, "Escape to Wisconsin." Dell had gutted the cart's rear and turned it into a bed for hauling items. Today it carried a bag of sand, a bag of gravel, and two shovels.

"I'm driving," Pike called out. "Let's go!"

So Corbett reluctantly descended the loft's ladder to find Pike, now seated behind the wheel. He climbed on to the passenger seat, and before he could voice any objection, they took off.

"We've got one of these, too," Pike said as he struggled to keep the wheel straight on the bumpy road. "But I never get to drive it," he sneered. "My sister—she's fourteen—always does." Then he hesitated as if he'd forgotten something. "Oh, yeah, I'm Pike."

"I'm Corbett."

"I've never heard that name before. It sounds very serious."

"It's a family name. My dad has it; my grandfather had it," Corbett replied. "I've never heard of anyone named Pike, either."

Pike smiled slyly and nodded. "My dad's kind of a hippie. Has to name everything after fishing. He's crazy about fishing. I mean my sister's name is Gil. So, what's your last name?"

"Griffith."

Pike nodded, looking deep in thought. "That's good."

Corbett shot a glance at Pike. *Glad you like it*, he thought to himself sarcastically.

As they drove past the pond Corbett had seen the day before, he noticed that large mound was still in the water.

"Hey, what is that?" he asked, pointing to the spot.

"That's a belly up beaver. It's been there a couple of days."

Corbett felt his stomach flip-flop. "I thought beavers were little. That's huge. So, they're just going to leave it there?" he asked, slightly disgusted by the idea.

"Yeah, I guess so." Pike shrugged, not seeming to see what the big deal was. "I think it's so big 'cause it's bloated."

"That's gross."

"Hold on!" Pike quickly warned, as they hit a pothole that hurled them off their seats and almost out of the cart.

Corbett couldn't believe he was riding around with this crazy kid in this crazy golf cart. He surprisingly liked it though. "That was fun," he exclaimed, laughing.

The two smiled at each other mischievously.

"Too bad this cart doesn't go faster," Pike said.

"Yeah," Corbett agreed and then pointed. "There's another one."

So down the road they went, weaving to hit potholes instead of weaving to avoid them and yelling out "Whoaaaaaa!" along the way.

"I think this is far enough," Pike finally said as he pulled the cart to a bumpy stop. "From here, we'll work our way back. Dell said he'd ask the Heffners up the road to take care of the rest."

Filling in potholes, Corbett found, was hard work. His dark brown hair stuck in clumps to his forehead, and sweat ran down his face as he shoveled load after load of gravel onto the road. He wished he had a bandana like Pike's and made a mental note to ask Uncle Dell about getting one.

After several breaks and a few exploratory trips into the woods, Pike and Corbett could finally see the culvert and pond again, which meant they were almost back to the lodge.

"I say the first thing we do when we're done is jump in the lake," Pike said as he parked the cart at the side of the road.

It sounded like a great idea to Corbett.

He was wiping off his forehead with the tail of his polo shirt when movement near the pond up ahead caught his eye. Something wasn't right.

"Hey, Pike. Look. That belly up beaver is gone."

"What?" Pike asked, looking up from his shoveling and over to the pond. He jumped up and down to get a better look. "That's weird. Where'd it go?" He dropped his shovel and began walking toward the pond. Corbett followed. Pike suddenly stopped short in the middle of the road and threw out his arm, forcing Corbett to stop short as well.

"Hey, what's wro …" Corbett started; then he saw what was wrong.

A bear. A very big bear was dragging the dead beaver out of the pond and up to the road.

"Wha, wha, wha what do we do?" Corbett stammered.

Pike shrugged. "Hope he doesn't see us?" he whispered.

Too late. The bear, with the beaver firmly in its mouth, turned its head to stare directly at them.

The boys gasped and stood paralyzed in the road.

"What do we do?" Corbett repeated anxiously.

"I think you're supposed to intimidate it. Try to look big and scary."

Corbett started to raise his arms, but Pike quickly stopped him.

"Maybe that's for mountain lions," he whispered, uncertainty in his voice. "I get them confused. One you're supposed to scare off, and the other you're supposed to slowly back away from."

Corbett simply stared at Pike, fear growing in his eyes. They were going to be eaten alive. He knew it. They were going to die!

Pike finally made a decision. "OK, here's what we do. Let's start backing up and try to get to the cart."

As the boys began to slowly step backward, the bear dropped the beaver, stood on its hind legs, and let out a roar.

Pike grabbed Corbett's arm. "Don't run," he ordered. "I know that much."

Corbett had no plans to run. His legs felt like Jell-O. This bear definitely did not look like a big black dog. He thought if he didn't pee his pants, he was going to pass out for sure.

Just then a ferocious growl filled the air. To the boys' shock, it didn't come from the bear. It came from inside the culvert.

"What was that?" Corbett asked, his knees buckling.

The bear obviously didn't want to find out. It dropped back on all fours and ran into the woods, leaving its beaver lunch behind.

The boys watched the bear take off.

"Run for the cart," Pike yelled, and he and Corbett bolted down the road and into the cart.

"I really wish this cart went faster now," Corbett gulped. They had to drive past the culvert and whatever was inside it to get back to the lodge.

"So do I," Pike said, "but I think we should go slowly and quietly—try not to disturb whatever's in there."

Corbett nodded in agreement, but then leaped out of the cart. He quickly grabbed a shovel they'd left lying in the road and leaped back in.

"Good idea," Pike said, smiling.

They slowly approached the culvert, their eyes glued on it, Corbett holding the shovel in a death grip. And there, standing in the culvert's opening, head cocked toward the road was … a dog—an ordinary mutt.

Pike laughed in relief. "It's a dog!" he exclaimed, as he stopped the cart and ran down to meet it.

"Don't!" Corbett called after him. "It could be dangerous and mean." Corbett wasn't relieved, and he wasn't leaving the cart.

"He doesn't look mean. He's wagging his tail." Pike bent down and started petting the dog. "Hey, boy. How's it going?" Pike looked up at Corbett. "Can you believe this scrawny little dog scared off that big ol' bear?"

Corbett looked back at Pike. He couldn't believe that Pike had obviously forgotten the trauma they had just been through.

Pike stuck his head in the culvert and growled, "Grrrrrr, ruff." The dog joined in, and their growling barks echoed loudly through the pipe. Pike laughed and laughed. "Dumb bear."

"That's great," Corbett announced impatiently, still gripping the shovel. "Can we get out of here before the dumb bear comes back for its lunch?"

"All right, Grif. Come on, boy," Pike called for the dog to follow him. "Can't leave our hero behind, right?"

"Whatever. I don't care. Let's just leave." Corbett paused then, furrowed his brow, and asked, "What did you call me?"

"Grif."

The dog jumped in the cart, lay down, and put his head on Corbett's lap.

"Look! He likes you!"

"Great. Now go!" Corbett ordered. "And my name is Corbett, not Grif."

"Whatever you say, Grif," Pike teased.

Back to the lodge they went, with a new friend in tow and with a story that brought Dell and several of the Whispering Pines guests back to the culvert to remove the bloated beaver and to fill in the remaining potholes. The boys got the rest of the day off to tell and retell their story. Everyone at Whispering Pines wanted to hear firsthand of the boys' adventure. Each time they retold the story, their stunned audience offered them a treat. Corbett had never felt so included in his whole life.

Later that afternoon, Corbett sat with the guest phone stuck to his ear, eagerly waiting for his dad to pick up. He'd been on hold for a while now.

Pike stuck his head in the lodge's lobby door. "Hurry it up," he called impatiently. "I've got a can of pop for you, and the Coopersmiths are making us sundaes," Pike continued and nodded for Corbett to come on.

"I want to tell my dad what happened," Corbett answered. "He's never gonna believe I came face-to-face with a bear! He'll want to hear this. I'm sure of it." But just then the line went dead. "I've been cut off," he said and hung up the phone. "I don't know why I bother." Corbett felt his whole body sag. He blinked back tears.

Pike started talking, quickly. "Hey, no worries, right? So, you tell your dad later."

Still hanging in the doorway, he nodded for Corbett to come again and flashed a big grin. "We've got Cabin 7 and Cabin 9 waiting to hear our harrowing tale. And I think I smelled blueberry pie coming from Cabin 11. I know they went blueberry picking this afternoon."

Pike raised his eyebrows up and down enticingly. Corbett laughed at that and headed for the door, smiling, the tears forgotten. He took the can of pop from Pike.

"I'm going to be as bloated as that beaver before the day's over!"

Out on the Lake, Part II

Bobby Lawless took off his jacket and shoved it into a plastic bag sitting on the bottom of the boat. He pushed up his shirtsleeves and adjusted his baseball cap. The morning fog was burning off the lake as the sun struggled to break through the hazy sky. It was warming up, and the scattered rays of sun twinkling on the water held promise of a beautiful July day. His brother, Blake, sat by the motor sipping coffee from a thermos. A couple of loons swam effortlessly a few yards away. The two men had been muskie fishing on Lost Land Lake since about 6:00 AM. The elusive fish had so far evaded them. On average, it could take an angler more than forty hours to catch the sleek, tube-shaped fish. Bobby cast his pole again, sending his feathery, six-inch-long lure flying through the sky.

"Do you see that?" Blake asked, pointing out from the bay they were anchored in toward the middle of the lake.

"See what?" Bobby replied.

"That eagle," Blake smirked. "It just tried to pick something up out of the water—something big, too big. It had to drop it."

Bobby strained to see what his brother was pointing at. "Man, you've got good eyes. Yeah, I see it."

Blake cranked up the motor. "Reel in. Let's have a look."

The eagle wasn't giving up easily on what it had hoped to be breakfast, and it tried to snatch the object out of the water again. Even the boat didn't frighten the bird away. It stayed, circling above.

"Would you look at that," Bobby exclaimed as the boat closed in. "That's got to be a walleye."

"No way," Blake cried. "Look at the size of it."

Bobby poked at the fish with his hand. It bobbed over, revealing a mammoth, milky white stomach. "Geez! Something bit it. Those are teeth marks."

He grabbed the net and scooped the fish out of the water. With its weight, it took two hands. The eagle let out an angry cry above.

"Sorry," Bobby said, looking apologetically up at the sky. "Man, this thing is ugly."

Blake cut the idling motor and got up to examine the fish.

It was grotesque looking, deformed by its size. The walleye measured twenty-six inches in length with a girth of thirteen inches and weighed about fifteen pounds. Its gills were still red, which meant it had been dead only a short time.

Blake shook his head in disgust. "Can you imagine catching that thing? What a waste."

"No kidding. But the bite marks, Blake. What could have done that?"

They both stared at the marks circling the walleye's belly. Obviously, there had been a violent struggle. Several of the puncture holes were ripped. This monster of a walleye had fought for its life against something very big. But what?

Bobby looked out across Lost Land Lake.

"Let's get this thing over to The Happy Hooker and get some answers. No one is going to believe this."

NAMES, NICKNAMES, AND MISCHIEF

The dead walleye the Lawless brothers brought in intrigued Corbett and created quite a buzz at The Happy Hooker. Fishermen were coming from all around to see the enormous fish now lying in state in one of the store's freezers. Pike's father planned to ship the fish off to a taxidermist for mounting after the ruckus died down and the Department of Natural Resources finished examining it. What killed the walleye was still a mystery. Corbett had no interest in fishing until he saw the walleye and its mouthful of thorny teeth. It looked prehistoric. And whatever had bitten it, he was sure, was bigger and meaner.

Just that morning, Corbett had begged Uncle Dell for a tackle box like Pike's—except, of course, Pike's would have a lot more gear in it. After Corbett had picked out his own box and a few shiny lures from The Happy Hooker, he and Pike sat on the lodge's screened porch sorting through their treasures. Pike was giving him a lesson on lures.

"This is a surface lure," Pike explained, holding up a bright blue fish. "I call it the Blue Bomber. Bass can't resist it. They'll hit it the minute it lands in the water." He stopped for a moment. "And northern pike. They'll hit it, too."

He picked up another lure.

"This," he said proudly, "I like to call the One-Armed Bandit. It's my best walleye lure." Pike held it up, his eyes glowing with admiration.

"You need a new one of those. That's taken a beating," Corbett said. Only a few scratches of black paint remained on its head, its feathery body was tangled, and the arm that held its single silver spinner was bent.

"And then some," Pike agreed. "I've got a new one somewhere." He rummaged through his tackle box. "Here. You can have this one, but not the One-Armed Bandit. It's got the scent."

"What scent?" Corbett asked.

"The scent of walleye weed. It calls to them."

Corbett rolled his eyes, and the two boys laughed. Corbett was learning that the fishing world was full of tall tales and teasing.

Just then, the boys heard a bark at the back door.

"Our hero is still here?" Pike questioned excitedly. He leaped up and opened the door, and in bounded a medium-sized dog with black, wavy fur. The dog had flecks of white above each eye and on his chin. It looked like he had two bushy eyebrows and a goatee, features that made him appear wise yet mischievous.

"I thought Dell was sending him to the pound."

"That's what he said. But he keeps putting out food and water. And yesterday, when we were in town, he bought a big bag of bones at the meat store." Corbett shrugged. "I guess we're keeping him."

The dog sat down next to Corbett, raised his bushy eyebrows, and barked again.

"You hungry?" Corbett asked, scratching the dog behind his ears. The little guy was actually growing on him. He got up to fill his bowl.

"We should name him, Grif," Pike called after him.

Corbett came back on the porch with a bowl full of dog food. "Would you quit calling me that," he said, exasperated. "The guests are starting to call me Grif now."

"Well, Corbett is just so serious," Pike explained, "like you should be wearing a suit or something. Horace Coopersmith, you know in Cabin 3? Everyone calls him Coop. That's where I got the idea. Your last name Griffith shortens to Grif. It's perfect."

"Well, my father doesn't like nicknames," Corbett said firmly. "He thinks they're silly, and *so* do I."

Pike shrugged. "OK. But I can't control what other people call you. So, what about him?" he asked, pointing at the dog, who was now lying down warming himself in a patch of sunlight.

Corbett returned to his tackle box. "I don't know."

He picked up a large torpedo lure with propellerlike spinners at each end and began twirling them as he thought about a name.

The propellers caught the sunlight that streamed in and sent it dancing across the porch. The movement startled the dog, and he jumped up and began barking and chasing the traveling light.

Pike picked up a lure and joined in the light show. The two boys laughed so hard their sides started to ache.

"I guess we know what to call him now," Pike said.

"Yep," Corbett nodded, "Spinner!"

Pike and Corbett were still on the porch when they heard two people talking and walking in their direction. Pike signaled Corbett to hush and lay low—the better to eavesdrop. Corbett recognized the voices as those of Vera Goodner from Cabin 5 and Uncle Dell.

"You know I don't interfere in other's business," Vera was saying, "but it's just not right."

Pike and Corbett quietly rolled their eyes at each other. Everyone knew Vera loved nothing more than interfering in other people's business.

"That Cabin 4 is jugging. Practically every night! And with that lady from the DNR boating around," she said this with slight disdain, "well, you could get in trouble."

Corbett looked at Pike. Pike shook his head dismissively and whispered, "Dell won't get in any trouble, but Taylor Wilson in Cabin 4 will." Pike held up his hand and rubbed his thumb across his fingers. "Big fine," he mouthed. Then he whispered again. "It's the DNR I'm worried about."

Obviously, so was Uncle Dell.

"So the DNR's been out on the lake?" he asked.

"Yes," Vera said sternly. "Not stopping anyone. Just looking around, it seems. A lot of gadgets in the boat. But that's not the problem here. The jugging. What are you going to do about that?"

"OK, Vera, I'll talk to him. Don't worry. And thanks for the information."

Corbett stared at his tackle box, deep in thought. *Why was the DNR patrolling Lost Land Lake? And why didn't Uncle Dell know about it? He knew everything. Maybe there was more to this monster walleye than was being told?*

"Oh, and Dell," Vera called, interrupting Corbett's thoughts. "That fish house needs a good cleaning. Cabin 10 had a run on crappie—must have caught over sixty of 'em down at the dam."

Just then a loud bang on the side of the porch startled Corbett. He and Pike jumped.

"You hear that, boys?" Uncle Dell yelled.

They did.

$$* \quad * \quad * \quad *$$

"So, what's jugging?" Corbett asked as the two boys made their way to the fish house.

"It's a lot of fun but illegal." Pike explained: "You take fishing line and tie hooks along it." He demonstrated with his hands. "So instead of one baited hook, you got a lot of baited hooks. Then you tie empty milk jugs to both ends and throw it in the water overnight." He paused and looked at Corbett. "You know, so it floats?" Corbett shook his head to confirm he got it. "The next morning you pull in your line and, ta da, you've got fish."

"Why is that illegal?" It didn't make any sense to Corbett. The object of fishing was to catch fish, after all, and jugging sounded like a great way to do it.

Pike shrugged. "Something about the sport of it. Not being fair to the fish, I guess."

Corbett shrugged back. It still made no sense.

Jill and Jenny Garfield from Cabin 10 were just leaving the fish house when the boys approached. The girls carried colanders stacked with fillets and swung their fillet knives as they walked. Corbett had little use for girls, but the Garfield sisters were different. Not only were they pretty and in high school but they baited their own hooks and cleaned their own fish. That was a wow in Corbett's book. He hadn't mastered either of those skills yet.

"Hi, guys. Sorry," Jill said. "The fish bins are overflowing. We've been cleaning fish for hours."

"Yeah," Jenny chimed in. "Our dad cut and ran—went up to the cabin for a Coke and never came back."

The girls exchanged a look.

"I tried to leave, too," Jill said sheepishly.

"But I wouldn't let her," Jenny finished. "No way I was going to get stuck in that smelly fish house by myself."

"You've got some nice fillets here," Pike said, examining the contents of the colanders.

Corbett pointed to Jenny's cheek and grimaced. "There's something on your face."

She reached up and flicked her cheek with her forefinger. "Scales," she replied annoyed. "They get everywhere. Did I get them all?"

Corbett nodded and then asked, "How many crappie did you catch?"

The girls looked like they'd just performed surgery. Their sweatshirts were splattered with blood.

"We've got fifty-three here," Jenny answered. "But we caught more—started throwing them back."

"It was soooo much fun," Jill gushed. "We were pulling them in left and right." She turned to Corbett. "You should get Dell to take you to the dam, Griffy. Or you can come with us next time."

Pike snickered. "He doesn't like to be called that."

"Called what? Griffy?"

"Well, Grif, Griffy. Anything but Corbett."

"Oh, I like Griffy," Jill said, smiling at Corbett.

"So do I," Jenny agreed. "It's cute."

Corbett's face felt blistering hot.

"He doesn't li—" An elbow in the ribs stopped Pike mid-sentence. "Ow."

"It's all right." Corbett smiled back shyly. "You can call me Griffy. I don't mind."

"Good. You let us know about the dam. Both of you," Jill said. "Our dad won't care if you come along."

"See you guys," Jenny said and gave them a quick wave.

The girls walked away, heading toward the freezer house where they would finish packaging their catch.

"Hey, Griffy," Pike teased and rolled his eyes. "At least I called you Grif. Geez, a couple of girls say you're cute, and bam, it's Corbett who?"

"They didn't say I was cute."

"Whatever, Grr-if-fy."

"Shut up," Corbett/Griffy commanded.

"Well, what about your dad?" Pike asked.

"I don't know." Corbett/Griffy shrugged. "He's not here. My name, my call. Right?" he asked with doubt.

"Right." Pike nodded his approval.

From that moment on, the name Corbett was forgotten. Everyone, at least in the state of Wisconsin, called him Griffy, and he made no objection.

A few minutes later, the boys stepped into the fish house. "Ugh! It stinks in here," Griffy cried out. He looked around the small structure. "This is creepy and so gross."

"What?" Pike asked. "It's not that bad."

The fish house sat on the banks of Lost Land Lake. Made of brown clapboard, it looked like a miniature cabin. The screened windows encircling the narrow building buzzed with flies and mosquitoes. Scalers, knives, skinners, and sharpening stones hung haphazardly around the room. The sink and wooden slab countertop were stained with blood. A large, bushy brush specked with fish scales and oozing slime sat to one side. A bare lightbulb surrounded by strings of novelty lights in the shape of sunfish hung from the ceiling. This touch of whimsy looked very out of place in a room that, to Griffy, resembled a torture chamber. The Garfield sisters had obviously cleaned up—the countertop had been wiped and sprayed down—but this place was beyond help. And the smell. *Whew!*

"What are you doing?" Griffy asked in horrified astonishment when he saw Pike sorting through the bins of dead fish and throwing skeletal remains and skins on the cement floor. "I'm not picking that up."

"Oh, quit being a wimp. I'm looking to see what people are catching. Look, here's a really nice northern." Pike held up a long, snakelike creature cleaned of its skin and meat. Its duckbill snout and tail remained intact, but its sides were gone. A thin layer of translucent meat held its rib cage and spine together.

"You can practically see right through it," Griffy said, amazed by the exposed veins and intestines. He actually took the fish from Pike, forgetting his squeamishness, and examined it.

"Uh-oh," Pike said. "Here are some bass heads. Someone is trying to be sneaky."

"What do you mean?"

"Bass aren't in season for another week. You're supposed to throw 'em back. Can't fool me. People chop up the heads thinking the fish will be more difficult to identify. But I know a bass when I see a bass."

"So, what's the big deal?" Griffy asked.

"If caught, you'll be fined—a lot of money. Just like jugging, it's illegal."

"There are a lot of rules around here," Griffy said, dismayed. He was becoming a little frightened to fish. What if he broke a rule he didn't even know about? He could be fined, or worse, arrested. What if he went to jail? He might never get to go home and see his parents again. "Maybe I shouldn't fish? With the DNR patrolling the lake and all."

"Don't be silly," Pike said dismissively. He took the northern back from Griffy and grinned. "I've got an idea." Pike's brown eyes had a sparkle in them that made Griffy a little nervous.

"Now what?" he asked.

39

Out on the Lake, Part III

Taylor Wilson hurried down to the bank of Lost Land Lake. He had overslept and was anxious to pull in his jugging line. He didn't want anyone to see what he was up to—especially Vera Goodner in Cabin 5. *The old bag*, he thought and harrumphed to himself. The day before he had pulled in a couple of nice bass and was hoping for more. In season or not, he was keeping them.

Rain drizzled down, making the ground slippery and the morning still. Years of erosion had exposed a maze of tree roots along the bay's bank. Taylor, in his rush, tripped on a root and slid down the embankment, smearing sandy mud down his right side along the way.

"Dang blast it!" he yelled as he came to a bumpy stop near the water's edge.

He'd chosen Whispering Pines Bay to jug in because it was hidden from view by two land points: Twin Pines on one side and Suicide Rock on the other. Boats had to slow down for safety when rounding either one, giving him plenty of time to hide his illegal endeavor. No cabins were in sight either. The closest was Cabin 5, which sat up the hill hidden by woods. The lodge sat on the opposite side near Suicide Rock. There, the woods had been cleared to make room for a dock and a good view of the lake. With the steady rain, Taylor thought, chances were slim he'd see anyone today.

Taylor stepped into the woods for a moment and then emerged with a long, thick stick that hooked at the end. He'd found it a few years back and considered it a vital piece of his fishing equipment. Every year, he hid it in the woods until he needed it. Taylor carefully shimmied his way along the bay's tree-covered shoreline until he spotted the first jug. Using the stick, he reached out, snagged the line and began pulling the jug toward him. Once he had the jug in hand, he began pulling in the fishing line tied to it.

"Hootie Hoo," Taylor called out as he saw his first catch: a two-pound catfish. It was followed by another, smaller catfish.

Then Taylor Wilson came face-to-face with something that startled him so much he let out a cry, slipped again, and landed bottom first in the rocky water.

A northern pike filleted clean on both sides hung from the third hook.

"What the …" Taylor exclaimed. Without bothering to get up, he pulled in more of the line. A bass head emerged from the water, then a dissected crappie.

Realization of what was going on slowly hit him. Someone had played a joke. Oh, yes. Someone had played a nasty little joke on him, and there was going to be hell to pay—no doubt about that. Taylor looked suspiciously around. No one. He was going to find out who did this and set them straight—guaranteed. His anger bubbled and quickly reached the boiling point as he realized there was nothing he could do, nothing he could say. Jugging was illegal, after all. At that thought, a frustrated Taylor Wilson got up and gave the milk jug now resting on the bank a hard kick. He then whirled around, looking warily down the bay toward Suicide Rock. Was that laughing he heard? And did he just see movement in the woods? *Naw,* Taylor thought, *it couldn't be.* His mind was playing tricks on him. He was alone. Wasn't he?

At the Dam

Their vacation over, the Garfield sisters had left Whispering Pines Lodge, but Griffy and Pike nevertheless found themselves at the dam. Uncle Dell said it would be a great place to teach Griffy the ins and outs of fishing. Anything could be caught at the dam. Its gates held back the mighty Chippewa Flowage, and when those gates opened, fish of any freshwater species could swim through and into the river below. You never knew what was going to show up on the end of your hook, Uncle Dell boasted.

Fishing poles bobbed up and down as the group made its way along the sandy path that followed the river and stopped at the rocky edge of the dam. Spinner led the way with Pike and Griffy close behind. Uncle Dell and Pike's father, Mitch, followed while Pike's sister, Gil, took up the rear. To avoid the swarming bugs, she had pulled her pink sweatshirt hood tightly around her face and walked looking straight down. Everyone had sprayed themselves head to toe with insect repellant before stepping foot on the path. As Uncle Dell warned, you'd be eaten alive without it.

The group emerged from the woods and began navigating the boulders and rocks that jutted out from the trees and into the water pooled near the dam's spillway. Gil let out a sudden shriek and dropped her tackle box. Its contents tumbled out.

Mitch turned back. "You all right? What happened?"

"A snake," she cried pointing to the rocks at her feet, "popped up out of that crack. A green one." She shivered.

Pike came running over. "Where? Where?" He squatted down and peered into the crack. "Nothing," he sighed, disappointed. He picked up a stick and started poking in the hole.

"Stop that!" Gil demanded. "You'll make it mad. Get out of there." And she gave her brother a shove with her foot.

"Hey, quit!" he yelled back, catching himself with his hand.

"Come on, Pike," his dad called. "Let it go. We've got to get across these rocks."

Dismayed, Corbett saw that crossing the rocks in question was the only way to get close to the dam's gatehouse. The group was now facing the overflow basin. The water here came from the spillway and flowed over a wide bed of rocks that connected to the river just below the dam's chutes. It created an island of sort out of the patch of land where they would be fishing. Uncle Dell told the group that they could fish off the banks of the river all day and never get a bite. But throw their lines into the chutes of the dam and, on a good day, fish would hit every time. Corbett knew he would be crossing those rocks whether he wanted to or not.

"We're in luck," Uncle Dell called out. "The gates are closed. Water's calm. Fishing's going to be good."

Gil stepped to the lead and, with a ballerina's grace, easily crossed the rocks and over the water that bubbled around them. She came to rest on the small island with barely a foot wet. Gil turned back as Spinner bounded through the six-inch-high water, passing up the others as they leaped from one rock to the next. Griffy nervously wobbled on an unstable rock, searching for his next move.

"Don't stop, Griffy. Keep moving," Gil instructed. "Jump to that brown one. Then to that spotted one."

Griffy nodded. He stared down at the rushing water. Uncertain of his chances, he took a deep breath and leaped anyway. To his surprise, he made it. That gave him a needed boost of confidence. But just when he was about to jump to the next rock, something splashed in the water to his left startling him. He tried to steady himself with his arms, but the fishing pole and small cooler he was carrying didn't help. One foot came off the rock and splashed into the cold water. He couldn't hold his balance, and the other foot soon splashed in, too. Griffy turned to see Uncle Dell helping Pike up out of the water.

"Not you, too," Uncle Dell cried, wiping his hands dry on his plaid cotton shirt. "Well, two wet feet are better than a whole body." Pike was soaked.

"The worms!" Gil yelled from shore. Pike had dropped them in his fall, and now the current carried the plastic container toward the river where it would be lost for sure. Gil bolted down to the river's edge to head it off. Luckily, the bait container became snagged between two rocks, and she nimbly maneuvered to retrieve it.

"Got 'em," she called holding the carton high.

Her dad waved back. "Good work, Gil."

Mitch and Dell had reached the dam, but Pike and Griffy were still in the water. They gave up on the rocks and decided, since they were already wet, to just wade across.

"Be careful, now. Watch your footing," Mitch told them. "It's still slippery, and it's hard enough getting across without carrying someone with a twisted ankle."

Damp and demoralized, Griffy finally made it safely to shore. His soaked shoes sloshed for the rest of the afternoon.

The group baited their poles and chose their fishing spots. Gil and Griffy sat atop the waist-high concrete wall overlooking the dam's chutes. Pike wanted to move around, so he stood with Mitch and Uncle Dell near the metal pilings that served as a barrier between the island and the water.

Dell brought in the first fish, a smallmouth bass. Pike quickly followed with a large crappie.

"Get the net! Get the net!" he called excitedly. "I don't want to lose this one."

Mitch came to his aid and scooped the fish up out of the water. Pike smiled triumphantly at his catch.

Spinner, appearing out of nowhere, tailed Pike to the fish basket. The dog barked enthusiastically when Pike dropped the flopping fish inside.

"Hey, hold on to that," Gil called. She had taken her sweatshirt hood down and tied her long, dark brown hair back with a pink bandana. "I've got one." She walked up holding an orange- and yellow-flecked pumpkinseed. The fish gave a sudden jerk before she reached the basket, and it fell to the ground. Gil bent down to retrieve the flip-flopping fish, but Spinner charged, knocking her out of the way. He scooped the fish up in his mouth and ran down the river's bank with it.

"Hey! Stop! Spinner get back here," she yelled and chased after the dog.

Not wanting to be left out, Griffy quickly went down to the water's edge.

"Did you see that?" Pike asked his face wrinkled in disbelief. "I've never seen a dog do that."

"Yep," Griffy nodded. "Spinner is definitely full of surprises."

The boys raced to join Gil in pursuit of the wily dog.

Spinner was not giving up the fish. He splashed in and out of the water. He paused briefly in the middle of the rock bed before running full blast between the three kids. He circled the island and came to rest near the fish basket. The three kids ran after him, almost crashing into Dell.

"Whoa, there." Uncle Dell grabbed Griffy by the shoulder. "You'd better check your pole, young man."

"What?" Griffy questioned. In all the excitement, he had forgotten that he hadn't reeled in his fishing pole. It was propped up against the concrete wall; its tip bobbed up and down. "I've got a fish!"

He grabbed the pole and started reeling in. The fish on the other end of the line didn't like that much and fought back vigorously. "It's a big one. I can hardly reel." Gritting his teeth, Griffy struggled against the weight of the fish. The tip of his pole dipped dangerously low. He pulled up and reeled faster. It dipped again. He pulled up again.

"What is it? What is it?" Pike asked, rushing with Gil to peer over the wall.

"Keep reeling, but keep it in the water," Uncle Dell instructed. "You don't want to break your line."

Griffy reeled and reeled until he finally brought the fighting fish to the surface. It was huge and ugly with large, gray scales and a lily-white belly. "Ugh! What is it?" Griffy asked.

"You caught a sucker," Pike answered, "the biggest one I've ever seen."

"It's a scavenger fish, a bottom-feeder," Uncle Dell explained as he reached down, grabbed the line, and pulled up the fish. "See its mouth." It was white and puffy and made a constant sucking motion. "Fun to catch, but not a keeper. Too boney. Here." Uncle Dell shoved the fish at Griffy. "Take it off the hook. Good practice."

Repulsed by the ugly, sucking fish, Griffy quickly stepped back. The fish fell and flipped itself off the hook.

Spinner, spying the much more lively prey, dropped Gil's pumpkinseed and chased after the sucker. He nipped at it, grabbed its tail, and shook.

"He thinks it's a chew toy," Griffy said, amazed.

"Well, he's not playing with *my* fish again," Gil said and ran to pick up her pumpkinseed. "Sorry about that, little guy," she apologized. Then she dropped the fish in the basket and the basket into the water.

About two frustrating hours later, Griffy picked up the worm container and sorted through it. Annoyed and disappointed, he was ready to give up on fishing. Everyone was having fun and catching fish but him. He had caught only two fish since the sucker, and he kept getting his lure snagged on the rocky bottom. He'd lost three lures before Uncle Dell had switched him to a hook. He'd lost two of those so far, one on a tree across the river.

Uncle Dell tried to cheer him up. "There's a knack to it, a feel," he explained. "You'll pick it up. Give it time."

Yeah, right, Griffy thought, and he watched Pike dodge Spinner as he carried another fish to the basket.

Griffy pouted. No one was even paying attention to him. They were all too busy casting and yelling at one another to stay out of their spot. *Typical*, he thought. He had been starting to feel like he belonged, that Uncle Dell and Pike really wanted to spend time with him. Now he felt like the invisible kid again.

Griffy put another worm on his hook and placed the container in the shade of the only tree on the small island. Bushes and underbrush surrounded the yellow birch.

The sound of cascading water drew Griffy's attention, so he ventured alone down a narrow, overgrown path that led to the dam's waterfall-like spillway and its overflow basin. It was much cooler on this side of the dam and a little spooky. The rushing water blocked out all other sound. Moist moss covered the ground and rocks. The overflow basin was strangely calm. Water bubbled only at the base of the waterfall and where it spilled over into the rock bed.

Griffy peered into the water. He could see mossy rocks covering the bottom for about three feet out and then nothing. *A drop-off*, he thought. It must be deep out there. He spotted a large rock about a foot off the bank. It looked like a good place to fish, so he stepped onto it and cast his pole toward the waterfall. He carefully cast between two concrete pilings that jutted into the basin from both sides of the spillway. He didn't want to get caught on one of those and lose his hook and worm again.

He reeled in his first cast. No bite. He cast again. Nothing. He wasn't paying attention, just sulking, on his third cast when he felt a tap, tap, tap on the end of his line. Griffy snapped to attention, but it was too late. He missed the fish. He cast again. Waited. Slowly reeled in. There it was again: tap, tap, tap. He jerked his pole. Missed it! Exasperated, he let out long sigh. Then he remembered what Uncle Dell had told him. "Let out your line until your bait hits the bottom; then reel in a couple times. That's where the fish are." So he cast out to the same spot again, let out a bunch of line, and waited. The line wouldn't go down—not enough anyway. He had too far to cast, but still when he reeled in, there was that same tap, tap, tap.

He needed to be farther out, closer to the waterfall. He looked up and down the short embankment. He didn't see another rock any farther out. *The cement piling*, Griffy thought. *That's the answer.* It was about a foot wide and about seven feet long. He could walk on that easily enough. But he couldn't see a way to get across the water to it.

Griffy walked over to the concrete wall that divided the gatehouse and the spillway. The piling dead-ended here. He saw a rock nested against the concrete wall about halfway between himself and the piling. It was too far to jump to, though. Griffy had an idea. He searched in the underbrush and found a good-sized rock. He dropped it near the wall close to the bank. He took a big step out onto it. It held, but the rock, covered in moss, was slippery, and Griffy lost his balance. Terrified at the thought of plunging into the murky water, Griffy flailed his arms wildly trying to save himself. He didn't know what the current in that drop-off was like or how strong it was. He could be dragged down, down, down. Using all his will and strength, he threw his body against the wall and hugged its cold cement tightly.

Whew! Close call. He would have to be much more careful. Griffy cautiously stepped back to shore, retrieved another rock, and dropped it in front of the first one. It held. He continued this, growing more confident each time, until his stone path reached the piling. By the time he placed the final rock, he barely had to touch the wall for balance. He came back to shore, grabbed his fishing pole, crossed the rocks again, and walked to the end of the piling. It was just wide enough for Griffy to walk on with ease. He glanced over his shoulder. Turning around was going to be a little tricky, but he'd manage.

Griffy cast out into his spot. Now it was just a few feet away. He let out his line, reeled in a couple times, and waited.

Tap, tap, tap.

He jerked on the pole. *Missed, darn it.* Whatever was out there was playing hard to get. He reeled in to check his worm. It looked good. He cast again.

Tap, tap, tap.

This time, Griffy didn't jerk; he waited—patiently. *Take it; take it,* he chanted to himself. When he thought the time was right, he gave the pole a slight jerk. The fish jerked back. He had it! Griffy eagerly reeled in. He didn't trust himself to bring the fish in on the narrow piling. It'd flip off the hook before he could get a hold of it for sure. So he kept it in the water, walking slowly with it down the piling, across the rocks, and to the shore where he brought the fish in.

Another ugly fish, he thought. He had no idea what it was. It had large, cloudy eyes with a dark green back, olive sides, and a long, spiny dorsal fin.

"Hey!" he yelled out. "I caught something! Ugly! Hey! Uncle Dell!"

No one answered. No one came. The rushing water muted his cries. Griffy shrugged. *Oh, well.* He was the invisible kid after all.

Griffy wasn't sure if this was another scavenger fish or a keeper. He took the fish off the hook and laid it in the underbrush for safekeeping. Griffy adjusted his worm and went back out to try again.

Tap, tap, tap.

This time, he knew exactly what to do and snagged the fish easily. "Ha! Got you!" he cried out. As Griffy turned around to bring the fish to shore, he stopped short. There, standing right in front of him and blocking his way was Spinner. Griffy hadn't heard the dog walk up behind him. *Oh no*, he thought and froze like a statue. He was afraid Spinner would start his fish grabbing game again and knock both of them off the narrow piling into the cold water below.

The two, neither one moving, just stared at each other. Then Spinner tilted his head to one side as if to ask: What?

"Back up," Griffy said and motioned slightly with his free hand. The dog, with an agility that shocked Griffy, quickly turned around and headed back to shore.

"Wow," Griffy sighed, relieved. "Crazy dog."

Griffy had caught another ugly fish with cloudy eyes: this one slightly smaller than the first. Spinner seemed to have no interest in the two fish lying in the tall grass, but Griffy was taking no chances.

He pointed his finger at the dog and commanded, "You leave these fish alone. Got it?"

Spinner just looked at him. He seemed to be smiling. The fish obviously weren't Spinner's concern. Griffy was.

Griffy shook his head. "Looks like I'm not invisible to you, huh?" And he gave Spinner a scratch behind the ear.

Griffy checked his bait situation. "We've got enough for another one. Let's go."

So Griffy went back out on the piling, Spinner following close behind.

Griffy cast out, but this time the tap, tap, tap never came. He cast again. Nothing. On his fourth cast, Griffy decided to give up.

"I guess there are no more ugly fish to be had," Griffy said to Spinner, and the two headed in.

Griffy took the overgrown path back to the dam's gates. He left the fish lying in the grass, afraid to pick them up. What if they were disgusting bottom-feeders or worse? He needed to find out.

"Hey! Hey! You guys! Uncle Dell!" he called as he made his way though the brush.

Uncle Dell met him at the head of the path, concern covering his face. "What were you doing over there? You need to stay where I can see you," he scolded.

"But I caught something."

"What?"

"I don't know. It's got weird eyes."

"Weird eyes, huh?" Uncle Dell questioned. "Well, show me."

Griffy readily obliged, taking Uncle Dell to the two fish lying side by side in the grass.

Dell let out a gasp.

That's not good, Griffy thought. "What? Bottom-feeders?" he asked.

"Oh, no. Those are walleyes. Behind a muskie, they're the most difficult fish to catch." Uncle Dell slapped Griffy on the back. "Two of them." He shook his head in amazement. "Good fishing. Good fishing."

Griffy smiled brightly and stood a little taller.

Uncle Dell looked around and asked, "Where did you catch them?"

"Out there, on that ledge."

Uncle Dell gasped again. This time, it really wasn't good. "No, no, not out on that ledge. That's too dangerous. Way too dangerous. What were you thinking?"

Griffy shrugged. "I dunno. It seemed like a good idea."

"How did you get out there?"

Griffy pointed to the rock path.

"OK, no harm done. Get those fish in the basket and in the water before their gills go pink. We're filleting those."

Griffy cradled the walleye in his arms and walked them to the basket. Mitch, Gil, and Pike were still fishing over the dam's gates, but the run had obviously ended. All were quiet.

"What'd you catch?" Mitch called over his shoulder as Griffy walked by.

"Walleye."

Mitch, Pike, and Gil jumped for a look.

"Good Gouda," Pike exclaimed.

"Sweet Brie, Griffy," Gil praised.

Amused, Griffy chuckled and pushed his way through the group. Being forbidden to swear by their parents, Pike and Gil used cheese for expletives or exclamations instead. They were from Wisconsin after all. Griffy, although used to hearing these phrases by now, still found it oddly funny.

"I've got to get them in the water," Griffy announced with an air of importance, "but I'll show you where I caught them."

"Bet you can't wait to tell your dad about this," Mitch said and gave Griffy a congratulatory pat on the back.

"Naw," Griffy replied. "He wouldn't be impressed. Not like Uncle Dell was."

"Or like us," Pike excitedly chimed in.

"Nope," Griffy smiled.

"Well, more bragging for us then," Mitch concluded.

When the four emerged from the overgrown path, they found Uncle Dell fishing out on the cement piling, Spinner sitting right behind him.

"Hey," Griffy scolded. "You said that was too dangerous."

Uncle Dell smiled back sheepishly. "Had to give it a try. Caught a bluegill the size of my hand but no walleye." He pointed down to Spinner. The dog had the fish in its mouth. "Take it on in, boy," Dell instructed, and Spinner turned around and took the fish to shore.

Once the two were back on land, Spinner dropped the fish at Dell's feet.

The kids stood in shock with their mouths hanging wide open.

"Pretty smart dog, eh?" Dell said and patted Spinner on the head.

"Only when he wants to be," Gil answered.

"Well, I think we should call it a day. What do you think, Mitch?" Dell asked.

"Sounds good. We've got a lot of fish to clean here, and it's after lunch already."

"But I want to fish out there!" Pike cried. "Come on, come on. Can't we stay?"

"Not this time, Pike. You can walk out, but that's it," his dad answered.

"Fine," Pike agreed, scowling.

Once the group returned to the car, Pike swore all to secrecy. "Not a word to anyone about where Griffy caught those walleye. That's Griffy's Walleye Hole. Got it? Anyone asks, he caught them somewhere on the lake, not at the dam." Pike looked over at Griffy. "We don't want anyone fishing in your spot."

Griffy nodded and smiled. *No more invisible kid*, he thought. *At least not here.*

THE DNR

The bell attached to the lodge's screened door clanked loudly as Taylor Wilson stormed in.

"It's gone!" he yelled and headed toward Dell, who was standing behind the register counter talking with Pike's dad and two people Griffy had just met that morning: Andy Gibson, head of the Chequamegon Lake Association, and Jo Patterson, a ranger with the Department of Natural Resources. They all turned toward Taylor. "My jugging line is gone. First, it was dead fish on the line. And now they took the whole thing!"

Pike and Griffy, who were playing bumper pool nearby, snickered.

Taylor snapped around and glared at them. He had stormed right past them, not noticing they were even in the lodge's lobby.

"So it was the two of you! I figured as much," he roared.

Fearful, the boys shook their heads no and quickly returned to their game of pool.

"Hold up there, Taylor," Dell intervened. "Now, what's going on?"

"I put a jugging line out last night, and this morning it was gone. Three days ago someone," he shot a look over to Pike and Griffy, "filled the line with dead fish."

At that, Mitch McKendrick, Pike's dad, had to stifle a laugh with his hand.

"The boys didn't take anything, not last night," Dell explained. "Mitch, here, took the two of them to an Indian powwow over at the Ojibwe casino. And this morning, we all had breakfast at Spider Lake Cafe, which is where we ran into Andy and Jo." Dell motioned toward the two others in the group. "Jo, by the way, is with the DNR. Jo, this is Taylor Wilson, a guest."

She smiled at Taylor. "I assume you know that jugging is illegal?"

"Yes, I know," he snapped back and then abruptly stopped. "You're with the what?" he asked.

"The DNR," Jo replied and pointed to the badge on her arm sleeve. "It's nice to meet you." She held her hand out to Taylor. He shook it in stunned silence. "I'd be grateful to whoever took your line, Mr. Wilson. They have saved you a hefty fine and the revoking of your fishing license. We don't allow jugging on these waters, as you know. But since it looks like the evidence has vanished, I'll let you off with a warning. How 'bout that?" She whipped out a pad and began writing. "Next time," she announced, handing a piece of paper to Taylor, "the fine will be double."

Taylor stammered a confused thank-you. Defeated, he gave Dell a final glare, muttered something unintelligible, and left the lodge.

"Dead fish on the line, Pike?" his dad questioned when Taylor was gone. "That had to be you."

"And Griffy," Pike replied quickly as he put the pool cues away.

Griffy's head shot up at the sound of his name. He had been examining a paperback on the overcrowded bookshelves. "It was his idea," he retorted, pointing at Pike.

"And it was a good one," Andy reassured them, grinning. He had been chewing on a piece of straw and now took it out of his mouth and pointed it at the boys. "Good work, both of you. I don't think Mr. Wilson will be jugging anytime soon."

Everyone laughed at that.

"So Lost Land Lake has another mystery," Andy continued. Griffy had heard his uncle talk a lot about Andy Gibson and the lake association president's zeal for promoting tourism. "Interesting, huh? Who—or maybe what—took the jugging line?"

"Let's not put the cart before the horse, Andy," Jo admonished. "It could have been anything."

"Like a gigantic muskie?" Andy taunted.

"A gigantic what?" Pike asked excitedly. He grabbed Griffy by the arm and pulled him over to the counter.

"Muskie. A seventy-pounder could very likely be roaming the waters out there."

Dell laughed and crossed his arms over his chest. "Seventy pounds? I don't think so. It would be over five feet long. Not possible. Not on Lost Land Lake."

"Well, that's what we came out here to talk about," Jo said. "It is a possibility. The evidence points toward it. The bite marks on that walleye for one. The jaw span of whatever killed it was about six and a half inches. Only a muskie can get that big. And there have been a few sightings, which we could chalk up to folklore, but ..." she hesitated, as if she wasn't sure she should continue.

Griffy stared at Jo and soaked in her words. Even he had heard the scary tales of a monster fish on Lost Land Lake. The folklore had frightened him, but Uncle Dell had eased his fears by assuring him the stories were just that—stories and nothing more. But now, here was Jo, a DNR ranger, making it all seem very real.

"But what?" Dell asked impatiently.

Jo bit her lip and looked at Andy, who was twirling that same piece of straw back and forth in his mouth. Andy nodded for her to continue. She sighed and went on.

"A seven-year-old girl over at Sunken Island almost drowned three days ago. Something grabbed hold of her leg while she was swimming and dragged her under and out into deeper water. Some teens sunbathing on a pontoon jumped in to help. No one saw what it was, though. There was too much commotion. Whatever it was let go. Scared off by the noise most likely."

"The bite mark on her thigh, Dell, only showed the front set of teeth," Andy interjected, excitement growing in his voice. "The jaw likely eclipsed the width of her thigh—so big all the teeth didn't take hold."

Griffy gasped.

"Don't worry," Pike assured him. "Muskies don't attack people."

"Oh, yes they do," Jo countered. "It's very rare, but muskies are voracious eaters and fierce predators. They possess an enormous mouth and strong canine teeth. They'll feast on anything—including other muskies. They'll attack ducks, frogs, muskrats, and humans."

This time Pike was the one who gasped.

"Why haven't I heard about this before now?" Mitch asked, his voice wavering. "Nothing much gets past me at The Happy Hooker."

"We've been keeping it quiet," Jo answered. "I didn't want swimmers to get hysterical until we knew for sure. Plus," she said, looking directly at Andy, "with a trophy fish of this size, well, we need to be prepared for chaos when the story breaks."

Griffy understood. Uncle Dell had given him books to read on game fishing. The ferocious muskellunge was the most sought after trophy fish in North America. If a fish of world record size was out there, it would draw fishermen—novices and pros—from across Wisconsin, maybe even the country. Chaos was an understatement.

"We need to look at this as a moneymaking opportunity," Andy urged with a gleam in his eye. "This could be big for the lake, very big."

"Yes, but what about safety? I've got swimmers here. Kids." Dell nervously adjusted the belt on his jeans and re-tucked the tail of his shirt.

"Exactly," Mitch agreed. "Folks need to know to stay out of the water. You can't keep a thing like this quiet."

"We don't plan to—not any longer," Jo assured them.

"There's going to be an association meeting," Andy explained. "I'm hoping for your support. Mitch, Dell, we need to turn this into a profit: sponsor a competition. I've got it all mapped out. It's a tourism gold mine."

"So it seems," Mitch said. "So long, peaceful summer. Well, let's hear what you got."

✳ ✳ ✳ ✳

Just before sunset, Pike and Griffy stood on the banks of Lost Land Lake surveying the water before them in awe.

"It's out there right now," Pike marveled. "Can you believe it?"

"No, it's too hard to imagine," Griffy answered as he stared at the water. Its surface was as smooth as glass. A monster fish swimming through that still water was unfathomable.

"We have to catch it. We just have to," Pike quietly pleaded. He seemed spellbound. "I can't do it alone, you know?"

Griffy nodded. He knew that, for Pike, catching a world record muskie was about the sport, the challenge, just because the fish was there. For him, it would be about something more. The task frightened him, but maybe, just maybe, if he caught that muskie, his parents—especially his father—would take notice.

"It's definitely going to take the two of us," Pike stated, "definitely. You in?" His brown eyes sparkled.

Griffy knew what he had to do. "Yep, I'm in."

THE MASTER
FISHERMAN MUSKIE
COMPETITION

The village of Minong, Griffy had discovered, was small in size but big in character. With a population of only 531, the village saw weekdays that were slow and lazy—the streets deserted, the air quiet. "Sorry, we're out. Be back at ?" signs often hung from shop doors down the village's small business strip. At first, Griffy had wondered how anyone could make a living in such a place.

Weekends. That was the answer. Minong woke up for weekends. Come Friday afternoon, the village came alive. It was time to say "good-bye, see you next year" to departing vacationers and "hello, welcome back" to arriving ones. Vacationers stocked up at Link Bros. Grocery for their weeklong stays and lined up for fishing licenses at the Sportsman's Headquarters. But the real action, Griffy now knew, was down on "the Strip."

On Friday afternoons, Main Street's three-block store-lined strip became a three-ring circus. Tourists eating ice cream cones at the Village Scoop passed the afternoon petting Rocky Road, the brown and black cow. Shoppers at Setting Sun Souvenirs got their pictures taken with Chief Running Deer, the ancient Ojibwe Indian who stood watch outside the store in buckskin and full headdress. Tourists passing by The Trading Post applauded the Indian brave and princess puppets dancing in the store's windows. Across the street, squealing children panned for fool's gold outside Hi Ho Silver, the village's silver and goldsmith. The smell of sweet treats lured tourists to the picture windows of Tremblay's Olde Tyme Candies to watch gray-haired Miss Gertrude stir a copper cauldron filled with boiling chocolate fudge. Next to her, teenagers wearing red and white striped shirts stood behind large marble tables mixing nuts into cooling batches of vanilla, maple, and chocolate fudge.

Tremblay's was the first stop Pike and Griffy made before heading to Minong Village Hall where the Chequamegon Lake Association was scheduled to meet. The McKendricks, Uncle Dell, and Griffy had come in town early to do some shopping and help set up for the meeting.

Like the tourists, Pike and Griffy paused before the candy store's picture windows before entering. Gil was already inside purchasing some peanut butter fudge balls. As Pike walked by, he pulled the strap of Gil's purse, causing it to fall off her shoulder and to the floor. Gil spun around, caught Pike by the tail of his shirt, and pulled—just enough to make him lose his balance. He instinctively reached out to grab something—anything—to regain it. What he grabbed was the arm of a young woman. The force of his grip caused the basket she held to spray jawbreakers and lemon drops across the room like bullets out of a machine gun. Customers ducked and cried out as flying candy pelted them.

Gil bent down to pick up her purse. Her face turned a bright red, and she winced slightly at the calamity she had just caused. She glanced up at the sixteen-year-old boy behind the counter and winced again, her face becoming even redder.

His face was bright red, too, from laughter. "You've got great reflexes," he said.

"Thanks," Gil answered with an embarrassed smile.

Griffy paid little attention to the commotion going on around him. He was still in awe. Tremblay's, he thought, was the closest he would ever get to a real-life Willy Wonka's Factory. The store in fact proclaimed itself "The sweetest place this side of heaven." Barrels filled to the rim with candy lined the store's walls. Bags of peanut brittle and almond bark lay stacked high on tables. Homemade chocolates crammed the counter shelves, behind which busy workers took fudge orders. Jars of gumdrops, rock candy, peppermint sticks, taffy, licorice, and much more filled the shelves. The store buzzed with constant activity. Everyone carried wicker baskets as they navigated the store and filled them to overflowing. The queue at the checkout counter never seemed to shorten as customers waited for their candy to be weighed and bagged. In the corner, a man kept the line entertained by banging out upbeat tunes on the piano.

What, Griffy thought, was the hands down best part? Free samples. Everywhere, free samples. They went fast but were replenished even faster. After four helpings of fudge, Griffy got a basket and got busy filling it. Pike was on his own.

An hour or so later, Griffy and Pike met up with Gil inside village hall to wait for the lake association meeting to start. The lobby was filling up, and talk of a killer fish circulated among the growing crowd.

Gil grabbed Pike's sack of candy.

"Sweet Brie! You've nearly eaten it all—in less than two hours," she exclaimed, shaking her head in disbelief. "Mom is going to kill you."

Pike grabbed the sack back. "I didn't mean to. We were just walking and talking."

"And eating. Don't forget eating," Gil chimed in.

Griffy looked into his bag. Just a few bull's-eyes, some fireballs, and a couple sticks of rock candy remained. This couldn't be good for him either, he thought.

When he and Pike had left Tremblay's, they'd killed time by walking through a nearby flea market. It was great fun looking at all the old junk while sampling their candy. From the looks of his bag, they'd obviously gotten a little carried away with the "sampling." When he looked up, fear filled his face as he saw Pike's mother making her way over to them. Luckily, someone walked up to greet her, delaying her for the moment. Griffy tugged on Pike's arm and nodded toward where his mother stood. "Your mom's coming."

"What!" Pike exclaimed, eyes darting across the room. He spotted her. "Oh no." In a panic, he grabbed Griffy by the arms. "Smell my breath."

"What?" Griffy winced and pulled back.

Pike shook him hard. "Smell my breath!" he demanded.

"Watermelon, OK. It smells like watermelon. What about mine?"

"Nothing." Pike paused. "But your tongue is blue," he continued in disgust. "We are doomed." He looked at Gil. "Stop laughing."

"Whatever," Gil replied, shaking her head in amusement. "How many times do I have to save your skin, huh?" She reached into her purse and then hesitated. She looked directly at Pike. "You are never to touch my purse again. Got it?" She drew out a pack of gum and held it out to Pike. When he grabbed for it, she quickly pulled it back. "Got it?"

"Yes, I've got it. Now give me the gum." He took a piece and gave the pack to Griffy.

"You two need to go back to Tremblay's and buy more candy before Mom finds out," Gil instructed.

"Mom will never let us go back there," Pike whined. Griffy nodded in agreement.

Gil rolled her eyes as if to say silly, silly boys. "Go tell Mom you are bored and want to go down to the pond. You know the one off the park out back? She'll say yes and then ask me to keep an eye on you. I'll cover. OK?"

"But we'll miss the meeting," Griffy whined. Pike nodded in agreement.

"Boys!" Gil exclaimed in exasperation. "You want something so bad, but yet you always do something stupid to mess it up. I don't know about you, Griffy, but when my mom finds out Pike ate an entire bag of candy, he won't be doing anything—including fishing—for a very long time."

"She's right," Pike said, grabbing Griffy by the arm. "Let's go."

* * * *

Gil saw Pike and Griffy coming down the street. She waved them into one of the village hall's side doors.

"About time," she said, holding the door open. "It took you long enough."

"We got a little sidetracked," Griffy replied, shooting a look at Pike.

"Figures."

"Mom been looking for us?" Pike quickly asked.

"No, she's been in the meeting the whole time."

"Good," he answered in relief.

"So? So? What's happening?" Griffy asked eagerly.

"Well, for one thing, our dad just nominated the three of us to pass out 'Swim at Your Own Risk' fliers. Can you believe that? I don't want to spend all summer circulating fliers. They are going to put up warning signs. I don't see the need for ..."

"Gil," Pike interrupted, "don't care about fliers. The competition—what's happening with the competition?"

"Fine, but you're not going to want to pass out fliers either."

Gil handed them an entry form that outlined the rules of the Master Fisherman Muskie Competition. Griffy read it out loud:

"All public boat launches on Lost Land Lake will be closed. Access to the lake will be limited to two points: Sunken Island Resort and The Happy Hooker. Whispering Pines Lodge will serve as competition headquarters. Competitors must check in at the lodge where they'll be assigned a launch site and time. No more than eighty competition boats will be allowed on the lake at any time. A safety check will be instated from noon to 2:00 PM and from midnight to 2:00 AM, during which all competition boats must leave the waters. The DNR and 'deputized' lake association members will be on patrol at all times. The twenty-five-dollar-per-fisherman entry fee includes one boat launch. Subsequent boat launches will be five dollars each. Lake residents and resort guests have free lake access if entered in the competition and can fish at any time—even during safety checks. The grand prize for landing the world record muskie: induction into the National Freshwater Fishing Hall of Fame, a permanent display in its museum, and five thousand dollars cash."

Looking up from the form, Griffy gulped, "Five thousand dollars? Wow." That kind of money would get his father's attention, big-time. If he could win five thousand dollars, his dad would be more than proud, he'd be impressed.

"Forget the five thousand bucks, Griffy," Pike blurted out. "How much money do you have?" He was sorting through his pockets. "I've got three dollars—maybe eight more at home."

"I've got two dollars here." Griffy held out a couple one-dollar bills. "Three dollars back at the lodge."

"Three! Just three!"

"Well, I've been buying souvenirs," Griffy explained. "I bought that tie-dyed T-shirt with the northern pike decal and that mosquito bandana, remember, and two rounds of candy." He shook his new Tremblay's bag at Pike.

"We've got only sixteen dollars." Pike hit his forehead with the palm of his hand. "We don't even have one entry fee! Plus we need to buy equipment. Our poles are too small to land a seventy-pound muskie. They'd break in two! Oh geez. Will Dell give you more money?"

"No way. I get an allowance every two weeks. The rest goes into a savings account so my mom can buy bonds for college."

Frustrated, Pike grabbed the top of his head and nodded. "I've got the same deal. What are we going to do? In two weeks time, someone could catch that fish."

Pike turned his head to look at Gil pleadingly.

"Hey, don't look at me. I'm not giving you any money. And I'm sure Mom and Dad won't either. It's going to be a madhouse out there. No way are they going to let the two of you enter. Safety checks: that's the only time you two are going to be out on the water."

"Yeah?" Pike countered. "What do you know?"

The brother and sister were about to go at it when Griffy spoke up.

"Fliers," he blurted out.

"What?" Gil and Pike answered in unison turning their hostile attitudes away from each other and toward Griffy.

"Fliers," he replied. "Didn't you say something about passing out fliers? Maybe there's some money in that?"

Gil shrugged.

Pike nodded and smiled. "Definitely."

GEARING UP

Gil drove the cart along the winding road near Sunken Island Resort as Griffy and Pike leaped in and out, poking fliers into mailboxes. Insects buzzed all around. Fed up with their constant assault on her, Gil grabbed a large fern frond from the side of the road to use as a swatter. She kept one hand on the wheel while the other hand waved the frond back and forth.

"Wave that thing this way," Griffy instructed as he hopped in the cart. Sweat trickled down his face. "Get that horsefly. He's driving me nuts!"

Gil swatted the fern down hard and fast, knocking the fly out of the air and onto the cart's dashboard. Griffy quickly smacked it again with his stack of fliers and flicked it into the road.

"Thanks. One down. Five hundred thousand to go," he said, feeling defeated.

Griffy examined the splat of blood and insect goo now stuck to one of his fliers. Oh, well, he shrugged. What could

Andy Gibson expect for ten dollars a week? Distributing these fliers was hot, hard work. They negotiated and negotiated, but he wouldn't budge from ten dollars a week per person. Griffy's enthusiasm over catching the mammoth muskie had not waned, but his enthusiasm over passing out fliers had. If not for Pike's zealous drive, Griffy would have given it up. A week to the day had passed since the launch of the Master Fisherman Muskie Competition, and he and Pike were as determined as ever to enter and win. The only obstacle still standing in the way: cash.

Pike walked up, keeping pace with the moving vehicle. A look of frustration covered his face.

"Even after we get paid today, we won't have enough money. Forty-six dollars. That's all. Not even enough for two entry fees. It will be two, maybe three, more weeks before we get paid again," he whined. "That muskie will be as good as caught by then. Have you seen all the boats out there?"

Griffy shook his head in agreement. "And more are coming in every day. It's amazing."

"Excuse me," Gil interjected. "Where did you learn to do math? You've only got thirty-six dollars. Sixteen plus ten plus ten equals thirty-six."

"Plus your ten equals forty-six."

"I'm not giving you my ten dollars."

"Come on, Gil!" Pike pleaded. "Why not? We'll give you a share of the five-thousand-dollar prize."

"You mean the one that you won't be winning? I'll pass on that."

"Griffy and I will catch that fish, guaranteed," Pike said confidently.

"You can't catch a fish if you don't have a pole in the water, and Mom will never let you out on that lake. It's crazy out there. Andy's called in the paramedics so many times they set up a permanent tent."

Pike looked like he was about ready to blow.

Griffy quickly interjected, trying to mollify him. "It's OK, Pike. You and I will pool our money. You can enter the competition now. We'll fish with what we've got. We'll use our next twenty dollars to buy better gear."

That wasn't going to mollify Pike. Not one bit. He fumed.

"You always ruin everything, Gil. What's wrong with you? Why are you being so mean?" He stopped walking, letting the cart pass him by. "I wish you weren't my sister! I wish I didn't have a sister!" he yelled after the cart.

Gil harrumphed. "I'm not giving you guys my ten dollars. No way."

Griffy shrugged and looked back at Pike, who now stood in the middle of the road, hands planted firmly on his hips, brow furrowed. "You should probably stop driving. He's not following us."

Gil kept her foot on the gas and stared intently at the road ahead.

"Aren't you going to stop?" Griffy asked, glancing over his shoulder and back at Pike, who was getting farther and farther away.

"I'm not giving *him* my money," Gil grunted, brow furrowed too.

Griffy sat back in the seat. "I give up."

Gil suddenly hit the brakes so hard the cart veered wildly to one side almost throwing Griffy out. Well, at least she decided to stop, Griffy thought as he rocked back into his seat.

"Nice driving," he finally said.

"Sorry about that," Gil replied. "But I've got an idea." She nodded to a rickety old mailbox sticking out of the woods just ahead of them. The peeling paint on its side read "T. Hanover."

Gil stood up and leaned out the side of the cart. "Hurry up, Pike, and get up here," she yelled down the road. "Come on, you big baby. Right here is the solution to your problem."

"I think," she whispered to Griffy.

With Pike begrudgingly back in the cart, Gil turned down the sandy road that curved through the woods to the neat but worn home of T. Hanover.

"Trust me, Pike. You are going to want to see this," Gil said as she struggled to dodge the branches and overgrowth that assaulted the cart.

"Whatever," he replied.

As the kids came barreling to the end of the road, they were greeted by a man standing—much as Pike had been a few minutes earlier—in the middle of it with his hands on his hips. Behind him stood a tan clapboard cabin, a garage, and two smaller outbuildings. In front of him sat a large German shepherd.

"What are you kids doing down here?" he demanded in a suspicious tone. "Turn right around now. You have no business here."

Gil gulped. "Mr. Hanover, I'm Gil McKendrick," she stammered. "My dad and I delivered groceries to you a while back." She got no reply or hint of recognition from Mr. Hanover. "Um, milk, eggs, beer. You were sick?" Still no recognition.

"OK, well, we are passing out these fliers." She handed him one, carefully avoiding the dog.

He glanced at it and handed it back.

"Young lady, don't do much swimmin' these days. Don't plan to start again anytime soon."

Pike and Griffy sat speechless in the cart staring up at the odd-looking man. Griffy had never seen anyone quite so old before. Only a few wisps of white hair covered his head. He wore eyeglasses as thick as Coke bottle glass. The huge lenses magnified his eyes to about three times their normal size. Brown age spots covered his arms and hands. His white T-shirt was clean, pressed, and neatly tucked into a pair of khaki work pants. A red and blue striped necktie served as his belt.

"Right," Gil answered. "We, um. Well, um. We …"

Keeping his eyes warily on Mr. Hanover and the dog, Pike leaned over to Gil. "Let's just get out of here, Gil. Come on."

Gil shot Pike an annoyed look and regained her composure. "No," she said firmly and turned her attention back to Mr. Hanover.

"Mr. Hanover, we are interested in purchasing some fishing equipment. My father bought some lures from you, remember? My brother and Griffy here want to catch this muskie." She shook the flier at him. "But they don't have the right gear to do it."

Mr. Hanover eyed the boys carefully. "Got one of those newfangled, ultralight poles, don't you?"

"Yes," Pike nodded. "It's not worth a thing, except for pan fish."

"Not worth a thing period," Mr. Hanover replied. "What about you, young man?" He nodded toward Griffy.

Griffy winced. "Worse. A hand-me-down ultralight."

Mr. Hanover laughed. "That is worse. Yes, siree." His demeanor softened, but he eyed them up and down just the same. "All righty. I think I can help you youngsters out." He motioned toward the garage. "Come on. And don't mind Sadie here," he instructed patting the German shepherd on the head. "She's harmless unless I yell sic."

Getting out of the cart, the kids followed Mr. Hanover and Sadie toward the garage. Mr. Hanover unlocked the door and stepped, with Sadie, into the darkness. A musty smell wafted out behind them.

Pike poked his head through the doorway and quickly pulled back. "I'm not going in there," he whispered. "It stinks, and I can't see a thing."

"Quit being difficult and come on," Gil ordered as she stepped into the garage and pulled a cowering Griffy in with her.

The three stayed huddled together in the darkness by the door. Griffy could hear Mr. Hanover shuffling around and mumbling to himself.

"Found one!" he finally called out, and a lightbulb blinked on.

The dim light revealed a makeshift warehouse. Aisles of shelves stretched the length and width of the garage. A series of bare lightbulbs dangling from the ceiling offered the only light. Pike saw another bulb a few steps ahead and quickly went to it. The cord was too high, but after a few jumps, he managed to grab it and turn it on.

Griffy and Pike let out a collective "wow" as they surveyed the room and its contents.

"See," Gil said smugly. "Told you."

The garage was packed with fishing, camping, and army supplies dating back to … well, way back. Griffy and Pike stood with their mouths agape as they stared at the boxes of tackle, racks of fishing poles, and bays of life jackets surrounding them. Knives, canteens, metal cookware, and all things related lined the shelves.

Pike grabbed a large wooden muskie lure. "This is marked five cents!" he exclaimed in disbelief.

Griffy and Pike exchanged quick smiles. Maybe, just maybe, their money would go a little further here.

"Where did all this stuff come from?" Griffy asked.

"Inventory," Mr. Hanover replied as he made his way back to them, wiping his sweaty brow with a handkerchief. "I was a shopkeeper as a young man. Opened up toward the end of the Great Depression. Now that took some moxie, I'll tell ya. Made a go of it too, but there was more money and fewer headaches in lumber. Always meant to reopen one day …" His voice trailed off, and he grew distant for a moment; then he snapped back. "Enough of that hoo-ha! It's hot in here. Let's get to finding you some gear. How big did you say this rogue muskie was?"

"They're saying seventy pounds or more," Griffy answered.

"Well now, that's bigger than the world record holder. Out on Lost Land Lake, you say?"

The three nodded in agreement.

"Haven't heard tale of that size since the glory days back in the late forties and then only on the Flowage." He paused for a moment and scratched his almost bald head. "You're going to need a pole with strength and stamina. Double-eyed cane. Yup. That's what you need." And he shuffled off.

The kids and Sadie followed him down one aisle, then another and then another. He finally stopped in front of a barrel filled with fishing poles of varying heights and widths.

"The best muskie men—your Cal Johnsons, your Louis Sprays," Mr. Hanover spoke as he sorted through the poles, "used something like this." And he pulled out a six-foot-tall, two-inch thick cane rod. "None of that newfangled graphite. This'll bring in the biggest, meanest fish." He handed the rod to Pike, grabbed a nearby stool, and climbed up to reach one of the shelves behind him. "Along with this," he said and threw two spools of fishing line down to Griffy and Gil. "That's Bailey's No. 5: the strongest, toughest line you'll find."

Mr. Hanover climbed off the stool and nodded his head at Pike, Griffy, and Gil as if to say they were done.

"Um, what about a reel?" Griffy asked impatiently. He was hot and sweaty and was ready to get out of there.

"Yes, yes, yes," Mr. Hanover replied hurriedly. "Can't forget the reel. Very important. The right drag and all. You've got to give a muskie some line."

He stood there shaking his finger at the three of them as if the movement helped him to think.

"A Kentucky reel should do nicely, and I don't mean the dance," he chuckled and shuffled off again.

Not understanding his humor, the three kids giggled and shrugged as they followed him once more.

Mr. Hanover turned down one aisle and then another, searching the shelves and yelling out the occasional "Confound it!"

The three kids moved up and down the aisles with him, marveling at all merchandise they were passing and coughing through all the dust they were scattering. Sadie had disappeared.

"It's amazing he can find anything in here," Griffy whispered.

Finally, Mr. Hanover stopped. "Ah, here it is. The Kentucky reel. Considered by many to be the finest ever made."

Pike examined the reel, gave it a few turns, checked the drag control, and nodded.

"It's real smooth," he said, turning the reel over and over and then passing it to Griffy. As the boys "oooohhhhed" and "ahhhhhed" over their new fishing gear, Gil got down to business.

"Mr. Hanover, this is all great. Thank you. But we don't have a lot of money—eleven dollars to be exact. This looks like old but expensive equipment." She hesitated. "We might be able to come up with more, but … well, how much is all this?"

"Not to worry, young lady. I was never one to swindle a customer. I figure what it was worth then, it's worth now. If you can part with nine of those dollars, we'll call it a deal and a day."

Gil shook her head. "Oh, that's not nearly en …"

"A deal and day it is," Pike quickly interjected, cutting Gil off. He shot Gil a look that said, "Are you nuts?"

She made a face back.

He counted out nine dollars and handed over the money. "Thank you so much, Mr. Hanover. This is the best."

Mr. Hanover clapped Pike and Griffy on the back and led them to the door. "Happy to oblige. Now, let's skedaddle. This place is due for a good airing out. I can hardly breathe."

They stepped out into what had become an overcast day.

"Better hurry on home," Mr. Hanover said, examining the sky. "Be careful, and happy hunting to you."

"Hunting?" Griffy questioned. "You mean fishing."

"Oh, no. I mean hunting. Muskies aren't called the Fish of Ten Thousand Casts for nothin'. And a fish the size you're hunting, that's one dangerous beast. Hold on a minute."

Mr. Hanover disappeared back into the garage and returned with a wooden club that he handed to Griffy.

"One last piece of equipment you'll be needing," he said, nodding to the club. "Free of charge."

"What are we suppose to do with that?" Pike asked.

"Hit the heck out of that muskie," Mr. Hanover replied.

The three kids looked at each other.

Mr. Hanover sighed. "You don't know what you're in for, do you? You haul in a seventy-pound muskie," he explained, "it's going to have a jaw span of about seven inches. Like this." He held his palms together and then opened them up. "That mouth is going to be filled with one fearsome set of teeth. We're talking teeth about one and a half inches long." Again he illustrated with his thumb and forefinger. "Think alligator. Think prehistoric beast. Think mean. In the old days, we all carried rifles in our boats and shot those ugly son of a guns the moment we landed them. But that, unfortunately, was outlawed back in '66." He paused and gave the three a good look up and down. "I'd never give you a gun anyway. You're all too young. That club is the next best thing. When you see that muskie, hit it and hit it hard."

Griffy stared at the club in his hands and shoved it at Pike.

"You take it."

Out on the Lake,
Part IV

It was a calm, sunny day out on Lost Land Lake. Although the waters were still, activity on the lake was not. The Master Fisherman Muskie Competition was in full force. Boats constantly pulled off the lake or launched on to it from the grounds of The Happy Hooker. Across the lake, Sunken Island Resort's boat launch saw the same chaotic traffic. The buzz of motors echoed around the lake as boats moved here and there and back again in search of the elusive fish.

Bob and Sheryl Dalton, up from Eau Claire to try their luck at the mysterious muskie, found a shady cove to anchor in. The couple broke for an early lunch after a disappointing morning out on Lost Land Lake. No one had caught so much as a glimpse of the mammoth muskie yet. A few stories floated around, but Bob Dalton was skeptical such a fish even existed. He took off his cap and wiped sweat off his brow and balding head with one swipe of his shirtsleeve. Sheryl unpacked the cooler filled with ham sandwiches, potato salad, chips, pop, and beer. Their boat sat half in the shade and half in the sun. She rolled her shorts a little higher, took a sandwich, and settled in for a bit of sunbathing. Bob grabbed a beer and began sorting through his tackle box. He had already thrown his favorite lures out there with no luck. As he sorted the lures, he hung them by their lethal, three-pronged hooks along the inside of the boat.

Sheryl, using her hand to block the bright sun, squinted at him. "I've told you, hanging them like that is dangerous, hon."

Bob waved her off. "It's fine."

Sheryl shrugged, closed her eyes, and went back to sunbathing.

She wasn't the only one catching a bit of sun that afternoon. For some unknown reason, muskies enjoy sunning themselves, and the rogue muskie roaming Lost Land Lake was no exception. The massive fish lay motionless a few feet away, its back almost out of the water.

Sheryl, finishing off her sandwich, decided she didn't want the last bite of crust. She tore it into small pieces and threw them out in the water for the bluegill to eat. The bread disappeared immediately.

Hmmmm, Sheryl thought. *Hungry little guys.* She grabbed bread from another sandwich and began tearing off pieces and lackadaisically tossing them out into the water. The first few she threw out like rocks skimming the water; then she began lobbing them high in the air.

Suddenly, the muskie, all five feet and seventy pounds of him, exploded out of the water. He snatched a piece of bread from the air, spun, and dropped back down creating a splash that soaked Sheryl and sent the boat rocking.

Wide-eyed, Sheryl sat in stunned silence with water dripping off her.

"What was that!" Bob yelled, looking wildly around. "Muskie?"

Sheryl slowly nodded yes.

"Where? Where?"

She pointed to the spot where the muskie had disappeared into the water.

Bob grabbed his pole and cast out. The large, green, gold-flecked lure sailed through the air, its spinner sparkling in the sun.

The muskie leaped out of the water, a picture of massive grace and agility. The fish engulfed the lure in its enormous mouth and crashed back into the water. Bob jerked the pole, trying to set the hook. But the muskie was having none of that. Poking its head just out of the water, the beast gave a wild jerk and spit the lure back out at Bob. He had no time to react. The mutilated lure's four-inch hook plunged into his thigh. Bob grabbed his leg in agony, lost his balance, and fell backward. He landed directly on the lures he had left hanging on the boat. No less than fifty hooks dug into his back and buttocks as he flipped over the side of the boat and into the water.

"Bob!" Sheryl screamed, finally emerging from her state of shock. She had only seen fish that size stuffed and on display in a museum. She had no idea a fish of that size could even exist these days. It was as long as she was tall! She lunged to where Bob had fallen in and found him struggling at the side of the boat. In his panic, he fought against the water, slapping at it as he tried to keep afloat.

"Calm down, Bob," Sheryl ordered from inside the boat. "It's OK. It's OK. Just tread water. That's it. That's it. Calm. Calm. Now move closer to the boat and give me your hand."

They locked arms. She was able to help pull him back on board. Bob rolled into the boat landing back first against one of the seats. He screamed out in pain. Those fifty hooks dug deeper, their barbs twisting in.

"I told you not to hang your lures like that," Sheryl scolded as Bob fell unconscious to the bottom of the boat.

$$* \quad * \quad * \quad *$$

The Daltons' muskie sighting sent the lake community and the Master Fisherman Muskie Competition into a furor. Carelessness caused by adrenaline and the excitement of landing the prizewinning fish sent many an angler to the paramedic's tent at Whispering Pines Lodge. Bob Dalton's excruciating, five-hour hospital stay, during which he had several hooks surgically removed, did little to calm the uproar. Even experienced fishermen and pros fell victim to injury, with devastating results.

Guide Sam Vonderbrink got hooked in the face when his fishing companion reared back to cast. Seven of the lure's hooks punctured his cheeks and lips before lodging themselves in his gums. Surgery was required.

Tournament fisherman John Clouse landed a forty-five-inch muskie, or maybe the muskie landed him. As John tried to unhook the fish, it flopped back into the water with John attached. The combative and cunning fish got away after ripping the lure out of John's hand and breaking the line. It took twenty-three stitches to close his wound.

The paramedics worked quickly and efficiently getting anglers back on the lake before the Novocain wore off, and their wounds' unbearable throbbing began.

Pike enjoyed stopping by the tent to deliver bottled water and other supplies. On any given day, he could see an eye laceration from a flying lure, a severed tendon from a fillet knife, or a hook embedded in someone's head. The grossest injury he saw was the end of a single two-inch hook sticking directly out from the center of one fisherman's eyeball.

Pike stared in horror at the man's eye. He jumped when he felt a hand clamp on his shoulder. "This is no place for kids," the paramedic told him. "Better move along."

Pike nodded in agreement.

Outside the tent, Pike contemplated the situation. It was going to take some fancy talking to get him and Griffy out on the lake. That was for sure.

OUT ON THE LAKE
AT LAST

Pike, scowling, shoved the cane fishing pole at Griffy. "Here, it's hopeless. That muskie's not in this bay. We need to be out there." He pointed to the middle of Lost Land Lake where about twenty boats jockeyed for position. "There's nothing here."

Pike's fancy talking, or begging and pleading, had gotten them no farther than the waters of Whispering Pines Bay. The deal the two had struck with Uncle Dell and Pike's parents restricted them to fishing the bay only, in a boat not much longer than the fish they were trying to catch—and with Pike's fourteen-year-old sister at its helm. The deal was not a very good one, Griffy thought, but at least he and Pike were now official entrants in the Master Fisherman Muskie Competition.

Pike had been standing and casting off the bow of the small, wooden boat that Uncle Dell had christened *The Lucky 13*.

Griffy learned that it once had ferried weekend sailors to and from their boat slips on Lake Superior near Duluth. Uncle Dell had discovered it at a flea market. He'd painted the dinghy white with red trim and named it after his favorite lure and the fact that the boat was number thirteen in the Whispering Pines fleet. Uncle Dell owned twelve other boats—one for each cabin. Two oars and a four-horsepower motor made it the perfect boat for fishing solo. But not today, Griffy thought. Today, it pulled triple duty with Gil, Pike, and Griffy on board.

Pike sat down in the boat, leaned back against the bow, and crossed his arms in frustration. He sat quietly for a change. He and Griffy had been fishing Whispering Pines Bay for ten days now: from the shore, off the pier, and with Gil in *The Lucky 13*. So far, nothing. Not one single tap on their muskie lure.

Griffy put the double-eyed cane pole and its gigantic lure aside while he reeled in his other fishing pole. He had pretty much given up on catching a muskie—any muskie. "Well, Gil and I are catching fish. Look!"

Both pulled in bluegill at the same time.

"We might have found the hole," Gil said smiling. She took her fish off the hook, then looked the boat up and down.

"Where's the fish basket?" she asked. After catching and releasing several tiny fish, she finally had a keeper.

The three looked around. No basket.

"You forgot the fish basket. Good going, Gil," Pike taunted.

"I didn't forget the fish basket. I don't even want to be out here," she huffed. "We might as well go in because I'm not sitting out here all afternoon just to throw everything I catch back in."

"We are not going in," Pike challenged.

"I'm in charge. I'm running the motor, and I say we are!"

"We're not!"

"You aren't even fishing," Gil answered smugly. "You're pouting like a baby."

"Am not."

"Are too."

Griffy's hand rose slowly in the air between them. In it, he waved a white fish stringer like a surrender flag.

"How about this?" he asked. "It was in my tackle box."

Gil, looking annoyed, grabbed it out of his hand. "It will do. But we *are* going to have to go in early," she said, staring directly at Pike. "Fish don't live as long on a stringer."

"Whatever," he replied and leaned back against the bow again.

At the bottom of Whispering Pines Bay, water began to swirl and spiral as a seventy-pound monster stirred among the weeds. The muskie, its green-gold body striped with dark vertical bars, opened its long snout as if yawning itself awake. Jagged, fanglike teeth tore at the weeds and small fish hiding in them before its jaws snapped tightly shut again. Propelled by the thrust of its massive tailfin, the muskie was off gliding effortlessly through the cool, clear lake waters in search of its next meal.

* * * *

"Can we move now please?" Pike begged.

"We're catching fish here," Gil stated matter-of-factly, "a real smorgasbord—bluegill, crappie, perch. Griffy even caught a catfish."

"I know that. But they are not the fish *we*," he pointed back and forth between himself and Griffy, "want."

"We found the hole, though," Gil fired back and looked to Griffy for support.

"Pike's right. Let's move." Griffy saw Gil's lips press together like a vise, but he kept talking. "I say on to fresh water before it's too late. We have to be back by dinner."

He and Pike had been trading fishing poles all afternoon. It would soon be his turn with the muskie pole again. He liked the power that came with wielding the six-foot pole and sending its large, dangerous lure flying across the lake. Eight inches long with a white body and red head, their plug lure carried four barbed treble hooks. The three-pronged hooks themselves were two inches long and two and a half inches wide. As the boys worked it through the water, the lure made a popping, chugging sound guaranteed—the packaging said—to attract fish.

"But," Gil started until Griffy and Pike interrupted her.

The two pleaded in unison, "Pleeeeeease."

Gil looked up at the sky. They were running out of time. "Oh, all right," she agreed. "Where to?"

"Twin Pines," Griffy announced quickly.

"Excellent choice, Grif. To Twin Pines, Captain," Pike ordered, and he began pulling up the anchor.

"No," Gil shook her head. In Whispering Pines Bay, Twin Pines was as far away from the lodge as they could get. "How about Suicide Rock? It's closer to home."

"Come on, Gil. Twin Pines. It's deeper over there," Griffy argued.

"But it is getting late …"

"And you are wasting our time," Pike finished for her.

Gil reeled in her pole and cast out again.

"Don't cast!" Pike yelled as he heaved the anchor into the boat. "We are moving. Get your pole out of the water."

Griffy was fed up with the constant bickering. Enough was enough.

"All we asked is to go across the bay. It's not that big of a deal. If you would have just started the motor, we could be halfway there by now. "

Pike looked at Griffy with surprise. Griffy usually stayed out of their arguments.

Gil started reeling faster. "Fine. We'll go. But I'm doing it for you, Griffy. Not Pike."

"I'm OK with that," Pike said smiling. "To Twin Pines it is."

Griffy was shocked Gil had actually given in again. That, like, never happened. Pike often joked about his sister's split personality. And, boy, was he right. Sometimes she watched their backs, and other times she stabbed right in them. Griffy chalked it up to her being a teenager and a girl.

Gil started the motor, turned the boat toward Twin Pines, and away they went.

About a third of the way there, Griffy noticed a dark trail of debris in the water behind them.

"Hey, what is that?" he asked pointing out to the water. "Gas leak?"

Gil looked over her shoulder and quickly cut the motor.

"I don't know."

She leaned over the back of the boat and peered down at the motor's propellers.

"It's not gas. It looks like … Oh nooooooooooo!" she cried. Gil reached over the side of the boat and pulled up the fish stringer. It and the fish it held had been chopped to pieces by the sharp blades of the motor.

"You forgot to bring the fish in?" Pike questioned, shaking his head in disbelief. He had moved from the front of the boat to the middle to get a better look. "Good going again."

Griffy and Gil looked at the fish stringer in dismay.

"You mean all of that," Griffy asked looking out behind the boat, "is blood and fish guts?" He grimaced.

"This is *not* my fault," Gil whined. "I cannot be responsible for everything. *We* all forgot to bring a fish basket, and you two wanted to go across the bay, not me."

She looked the bloody, mangled stringer up and down. "Poor, poor fish."

Their catch of a dozen or so fish had been reduced to about three. Mutilated parts—heads, gills, fins, and flesh—hung haphazardly from the frayed stringer.

"Well, look on the bright side," Griffy said. "We won't have to clean them. That fish house creeps me out."

"*That* is creeping me out," Pike chimed in, pointing to the stringer. "Drop that thing back in the water." Standing, he cast the double-eyed cane, letting the muskie lure fly past the back of the boat. It dropped right in the middle of the trail of guts and blood.

Gil put what was left of the stringer back in the water. She and Griffy sat in depressed silence, staring at the spot where the knotted stringer was tied to the boat.

Suddenly, *The Lucky 13* rocked sharply to the right. The jolt threw Griffy off his seat. Pike, who was standing, fell backward and nearly went overboard. He, Griffy, and the muskie pole all landed at the bottom of the boat. Gil barely stayed seated.

"What was that!" she shouted when the boat righted itself. "Did we hit something? It felt like we hit something? Did we hit something?" She looked wildly at the water surrounding them.

Pike pulled himself up. Griffy stayed where he was.

"We aren't moving, Gil," Pike answered. "Something hit us." He leaned over the side of the boat, searching the water.

"Don't do that!" Griffy yelled at Pike. From his spot on the bottom of the boat, he grabbed Pike's shirt and pulled him back. "Do you want to fall in?"

Just as Griffy said that, *The Lucky 13* rocked violently to the right again.

"Holy chedda cheese," Pike called out as he found himself on the bottom of the boat again.

All three now sat with their rear ends firmly planted on the bottom of *The Lucky 13* and their hands clutching both sides of it. No one said a word. They just rocked back and forth with the boat, waiting.

Gil was the first to break the long silence. She began to quietly sing: "Don't rock the boat. Don't rock the boat, baby."

Pike joined in: "Don't rock the boat. Don't tip the boat over. Don't rock the booooo-oh-oh-oh-oat."

"Funny, guys." Griffy smiled in spite of his fear. He was thankful for the comic relief.

As the boat's wild rocking calmed, so did the kids, and they pulled themselves back onto their seats.

"I don't know what that was, and I don't want to find out," Gil said. "Let's get out of here."

"I second that," Griffy said.

"It's unanimous then." Pike nodded.

As Gill turned to start the motor, she stopped short. "Good Gouda," she gasped.

"What? What is it?" Pike asked, his voice raising an octave. From his seat at the bow, he strained to see what was going on.

"The stringer. It's gone."

She untied what was left of the stringer and held it out for Pike and Griffy to see.

"It looks like it's been cut," Griffy exclaimed. "How …"

The three surveyed the water around them, fear growing on their faces.

"Vamanos, Gil. Vamanos," Pike ordered.

She jumped to action, cranked up the motor, and turned the boat toward the lodge and Suicide Rock. Luckily, the rocking boat had moved them a little closer to home.

The Lucky 13 sped—as fast as a four-horsepower motor allowed—for the dock at Whispering Pines Lodge. They almost made it, too, but the muskie pole, resting against the side of the boat, suddenly slipped and caught on the underside of Griffy's seat.

"Whoaaaaa, Gil. Whoaaaaa," Pike called, waving his hands back and forth over his head.

Gil cut the motor.

"Muskie pole's still in the water," Griffy explained as he reached down to dislodge the reel. As soon as he got it free, the pole jerked sharply backward. Griffy wrestled it with both hands before being pulled spread eagle toward the stern of the boat.

With only seconds to react, Gil jumped away from the motor as Griffy and the fishing pole flew at her. As it had with the muskie pole, Griffy's bench seat stopped him. His feet caught on its side saving him from being pulled out of the boat.

"Hit the drag! Hit the drag! Give it line!" Pike ordered.

But Griffy couldn't move. All he could do was hold on.

"Don't let go, Grif!" Pike pleaded as he leaped to Griffy's aid.

With one hand, he grabbed the muskie pole just above the reel. With the other, he pushed the drag button and released the line. He wasn't quick enough to save Griffy, though. With the tension gone, Griffy dropped—KERPLUNK!—to the bottom of the boat.

"Sorry, dude," Pike winced as he took the fishing pole from Griffy.

Griffy moaned and pulled himself up. He flexed his hands back and forth. They hurt, bad.

"Do you think we snagged a log?" Gil asked quietly as she settled back in at the boat's helm.

"I don't know," Pike answered. He started reeling the line in. "We'll soon see."

Griffy watched Pike in tense silence.

With the pole held high, Pike reeled and reeled. He heaved the pole back. It bent dangerously low. "Ugh," he gasped. "It feels like a log—dead weight—but it's moving." He kept reeling, but it was difficult and slow going. "Here, my arms are killing me," Pike said, passing the pole to Griffy.

"Geez!" Griffy exclaimed. "It weighs a ton." He reeled and reeled, heaved and heaved working the log closer and closer to the boat.

"Let's just cut the line and go in," Gil stated. Her hands were shaking.

"Take over, Pike," Griffy called out. "My arms are about ready to go."

Pike grabbed the pole and started reeling again. Strangely, the line became very slack, gathering in curls at the water's surface.

"Hey, I think we lost it," Pike announced and reeled faster.

Curious, both Gil and Griffy peered into the water.

"I don't see anything," Gil said.

She spoke too soon.

A flat, reptilianlike head almost as big as hers broke water about four feet from the boat. The beady-eyed muskie flashed its cream-colored belly and then disappeared.

"Ohmigod!" Gil gasped.

"Did you see it! Did you see it?! What was it?" Griffy shouted.

Pike stopped reeling. "Mu-u-uskie," he stammered.

Somehow, seeing the five-foot monster muskie didn't frighten Griffy as much as it excited him. He yelled at Pike and Gil. "Wow! Did you see it?" He punched Pike in the arm. "Keep reeling! Keep reeling!"

The punch seemed to get Pike back on track and in fisherman mode. He quickly got the slack out of the line and gave the pole a heave. The muskie, playing dead before, came alive. It frantically jumped out of the water and flipped violently in the air, trying to free itself from the lure lodged in its mouth. Its massive body crashed back down, spraying the kids and *The Lucky 13* with cold lake water.

"HOLY CHEDDA CHEESE!" Pike and Griffy yelled.

95

Gil didn't ask anyone's permission this time. She sat down at the motor and cranked it up. She was getting out of there—fish or no fish. Out of the corner of his eye, Griffy saw Gil pick up the wooden club that Mr. Hanover had given them. "When you see that muskie, hit it and hit it hard," he had told them. Griffy saw her place the club's leather strap around her wrist and, with her other hand, grab the handle of the idling motor.

"Brace yourselves, boys," she warned. "We're going in."

Pike and Griffy battled the muskie as Gil inched them closer and closer to shore. The muskie fought vigorously now. The small motor was barely a match for it. The fish kept pulling the boat sideways.

"The pole's holding up. The line's holding up. Our only hope is to wear him down," Pike instructed as he wiped sweat off his face and onto his T-shirt. The double-eyed cane pole showed amazing flexibility against the muskie's weight. Griffy didn't know how much longer he could battle this monster. His arms ached. The thought of winning that five-thousand-dollar prize and showing his dad was all that kept him going.

Gil seemed to have her own agenda. "I see bottom!" she yelled. She cut the motor, grabbed the anchor's rope, and jumped out of the boat."

"Gil! Are you crazy!" Pike screamed after her. "You'll drown."

"Will not! I've got a life jacket on. Duh. I'm anchoring us on shore."

She took a couple determined steps through the shoulder-high water, but without the pull of the motor fighting against it, the muskie was too strong. The fighting fish pulled her and *The Lucky 13* into deeper water. Griffy noticed Gil treading water instead of walking. She obviously couldn't touch bottom anymore. The anchor looked like it weighed a ton.

"Hold on, Gil," Griffy commanded. He passed the pole once again to Pike and readied the oars.

Griffy oared with all his might, trying to push *The Lucky 13* back to shallow water. With Gil kicking hard and fast, she was soon able to stand again. She lowered her head and, with determination, began dragging the anchor to shore. Griffy stopped oaring and instead used one of the paddles as a wedge. Digging it into the lake's bottom, he pushed off again and again with as much force as he could muster. Gil struggled against the now waste-high water, lunging herself closer and closer to shore.

Underwater, less than seven feet from *The Lucky 13*, the muskie whipped its head back and forth trying once more to dislodge the lure implanted in its mouth. *Go deep*, its instincts said. But the muskie couldn't. The water was too shallow. *Find a weed bed*. But in this part of the bay, the weeds weren't plentiful enough for a five-foot, seventy-pound fish to tangle itself up in. *Get to open water*. But whatever had hold of it wasn't letting that happen. *Escape*, its instincts cried out. *Find a way to escape. Any way.* So the muskie changed its tactics. The massive beast turned away from the depths of Lost Land Lake and swam with torpedolike speed toward the bottom of *The Lucky 13*.

* * * *

One final lunge put Gil safely on shore. She ran to the nearest tree and swung the anchor around its trunk. Gil wrapped the end of the twenty-five-foot rope around several times to secure it.

"OK. Anchor secure!" she yelled as she gave it one last tug. Gil turned back toward the boat and gave Pike and Griffy the thumbs-up signal. Griffy waved back and put his oar down.

Gil sighed with relief and sat down on the rocky shore. Now all Pike and Griffy had to do was wear that muskie down.

But the kids didn't know that muskies never gave up a fight—ever. Giving up wasn't in their predatory nature. As Gil rested on shore, the massive fish sped toward *The Lucky 13* and hit it with such force the small boat capsized.

Griffy never saw it coming, and he was sure that Pike hadn't either. The boys barely had time to scream before being thrown out of the boat and into the water.

Griffy's life jacket did its job, and he quickly resurfaced unharmed. Relieved, he saw that Pike had come up, too. Standing in the chest-high water, Pike looked at his hands in dismay.

"The pole! The pole!" he panicked. "I dropped the pole! Griffy! Help!"

Both boys looked down, searching the water frantically.

"I don't see it! I don't see it!" Pike cried out.

Simultaneously, the boys removed their life jackets and dove underwater.

$$* \quad * \quad * \quad *$$

During the commotion following *The Lucky 13*'s capsize, the muskie readied for another attack. It swam under the lodge's dock and circled back. In doing so, it wrapped the fishing line around one of the dock's posts, snapping the line and setting the ferocious beast free. If the fish knew it was free to swim away, it gave no indication. It was a predator, and its prey was in the water just a few feet away.

＊　＊　＊　＊

Griffy came up for air briefly, then dove underwater again. He spied the cane pole and needed a little more air to retrieve it. Breaststroking through the water, he snatched the pole and prepared to resurface when movement caught his eye. The muskie swam past him with a force that sent waves through the water. Griffy bobbed backward against it and watched in horror as the beast headed for Pike. The fish's stalking pattern made Griffy think of a wolf, a long, spearlike wolf hunting the waters.

Griffy swam underwater toward Pike but had to resurface when his lungs felt they would burst. He saw that Pike had resurfaced near the dock in waist-high water. Griffy held up the pole and yelled, "Pike! Look out! Get out of the water!"

But Pike didn't seem to hear or see him. He appeared to be in a trance, staring blankly at the cane pole and the broken fishing line fluttering in the sky.

"Pike!" Griffy screamed again waving his arms and the pole back and forth. "Muskie coming! Move! Now!"

Pike's face finally wrinkled in puzzlement. "What?"

Too late.

Pike let out an agonizing yelp as the muskie, with a fast, powerful lunge, sank its razor-sharp fangs into his thigh. He fell back into the water. Streams of blood rose to the surface.

Griffy struggled against the weight of the water to reach his friend. He saw Gil racing into the water from shore to help. Griffy reached Pike first; he jabbed the muskie with the bottom of the double-eyed cane and pulled Pike, gasping for air, up out of the water.

The muskie didn't let go. Instead, it whipped its sleek body around and stabbed Griffy's arm with one of its spiky side fins. Blood oozed down his arm, but Griffy didn't let go either. He locked his hands and arms around Pike's chest. With all the might he could gather, Griffy slowly heaved Pike and the muskie clamped on his leg into shallower water.

The muskie shook its head frenetically. Pike screamed in pain as his puncture wounds ripped wider. Griffy lost his footing, fell backward, and landed on the lake's bottom. Gil reached the scene just as Griffy went under water, trapped by the muskie and Pike's body. Struggling to keep his face above water, Griffy motioned toward the cane pole. "Grab the pole and jab!" he ordered.

Gil stabbed the monster fish as its tail whipped violently side to side. "BACK OFF MY BROTHER!" she screamed.

Her blows helped Griffy escape, but still the beast held on to Pike. As Griffy struggled to regain his footing, he had an idea.

"The club! The club! Where is it?"

Gil looked confused for a moment and then exclaimed, "It's here! I forgot!" She had run from shore with the club Mr. Hanover had given them still strapped on her wrist.

Gil thrust the club at Griffy. With both hands, he raised it high overhead and swung down hard striking the scaly monster right between its beady eyes. He raised his arms and swung again. Splat! Bam!

The heavy blows dazed the beast but did little to loosen its grip on Pike's leg. Griffy and Gil grabbed Pike and dragged him and the semiconscious fish closer to shore. As the lake water receded around it, the muskie seemed to find a new life. It released Pike and thrashed out of control in the now knee-deep water. Its long, lean tubular body flipped and jerked in a fierce show of aerial acrobatics. Its fanlike tailfin and sharp side fins sliced at Pike, Griffy, and Gil as they rolled, jumped, and dragged themselves out of the crazed animal's destructive path.

Then, out of nowhere, Spinner came running full speed down the Whispering Pines dock. In an aerial show of his own, Spinner leaped from the dock and flew through the air landing directly on the muskie. He sank his teeth into the muskie's spine, partially paralyzing the beast. Its mighty tail no longer fully functioning, the fish rolled violently side to side trying to shake Spinner off. But the dog held on and actually seemed to enjoy the turbulent ride.

Spinner gave the kids their chance, and they pounced. Gil seized the cane pole and jabbed the fish over and over. Griffy clubbed it again and again. Pike, despite his injured leg, ensnared the muskie in fishing line.

When the massive fish finally lay lifeless, the kids and Spinner began dragging its seventy-pound body inch by inch to shore.

It was over.

Gil, Pike, Griffy, and the muskie—with Spinner nipping at its tail—lay together on the rocky shoreline.

"What the heck is going on here?"

Griffy looked up weakly and saw Andy Gibson approaching. He stopped at the top of the embankment, hands on his hips, and looked down.

"We can hear you guys all the way over," he continued scolding until he saw them. "What the ...?"

Griffy knew the scene must have looked ugly. There was Gil, stretched out and holding onto a double-eyed cane pole. There was Pike, lying on his side, bleeding and ensnarled in fishing line. There he was, hugging a club to his chest and chanting softly, "We got him. We got him." And in between them was a prehistoric-looking monster fish—dead, dead at last.

Spinner barked wildly at Andy, placed both paws on the muskie, and hunkered down, guarding their catch.

Andy grabbed his walkie-talkie as he raced down the embankment. "I need the medics ASAP at the bay. And get Dell. Over."

MASTER FISHERMEN

Griffy could hardly wait to see the morning paper. He and Pike huddled around it, both holding up a side. "Kids Dethrone Freshwater King," *The Minong Ledger*'s front-page headline proclaimed. The picture accompanying the article showed the five-foot, seventy-pound muskie winched high in the air by its snout. Pike and Griffy flanked "the King" on each side with Gil kneeling in front holding Spinner.

Griffy smiled broadly.

"Look at us," Pike gushed. He blew on his knuckles and wiped them on his shirt with pride. "We're celebrities."

"Famous, even," Griffy raved.

"Don't let it go to your heads," Gil admonished as she walked up behind them. She took a look at the newspaper.

"Wow, we are famous," she gasped happily.

And their fame grew in the days following the muskie's heroic capture. Griffy couldn't believe all the people who wanted autographs or pictures taken with them. Everywhere they went, folks clapped them on the back, shook their hands, and asked to hear about their battle with the ferocious beast and to see their battle wounds. Griffy showed off the twelve stitches in his arm. Pike, on crutches, received more sympathy for his stitched-up, bandaged-up thigh.

Even more, to Griffy's amazement, Minong organized its first Muskie Festival, complete with a muskie queen and court, in honor of the town's newly proclaimed master fishermen. Taxidermists worked day and night preparing a replica of the giant muskie for the festival's opening parade. Pike, Gil, and Griffy nervously watched as hundreds of people turned out and stood five deep to see the two-hour event.

"Can you believe all these people are here for us?" Gil asked in awe.

No more invisible kid, Griffy thought. Now he had more attention than he'd ever imagined. And his mom had sounded proud of him when he'd called and told her about battling the muskie and saving Pike. She really had. There was only one problem.

"Hey, look there!" His thoughts were interrupted by Gil blurting out, "It's Mr. Hanover."

The three kids rushed through the crowd to greet him.

"Well, you caught yourselves a humdinger. Yes, siree. Louis Spray couldn't have done better himself!" Mr. Hanover shook his head in amazement.

"We couldn't have done it without you, Mr. Hanover," Pike acknowledged.

"Nonsense," Mr. Hanover countered. "Equipment's not even half of it. Skill won't even get you there. It's moxie. And the three of you've got buckets of it."

Gil, Pike, and Griffy laughed at that and thanked Mr. Hanover for the compliment.

"So, now, son." Mr. Hanover turned his attention to Griffy. "This has got to be an extra special day for you. First trip to Wisconsin and already in the hall of fame. Where are those folks of yours? I'd like to congratulate them."

"They're not here. They're in Chicago," Griffy replied. "Too busy to make it up."

"Well, I've never heard of such a thing," Mr. Hanover huffed. "That's a load of hooey if you ask me."

"They've got deadlines, meetings, business trips," Pike explained, "that sort of thing."

Griffy smiled sadly and shook his head. "Naw. That's really not it. Thanks, Pike." He knew his friend was trying to help him. "Bottom line is they're just not interested. Not in me. Not in what I do. They were excited on the phone, and that's good enough—for now. Maybe someday I'll do something worthwhile to them."

"Someday! Someday!" Mr. Hanover cried out in disbelief. "I don't come to town for just anyone, young man. You are worthwhile now. And don't you forget it. It's not your fault your parents are too blind to see it."

"That's true, Griffy." Gil nodded. "Who needs parents when you've got us and a few dozen cheerleaders?" She pointed toward several groups of teenage girls with short skirts and pom-poms making their way through the crowd.

"Oh no! We're gonna be late," Pike gasped. "The parade's about to start."

"Get yourselves going then," Mr. Hanover ordered with a smile and waved them good-bye.

Griffy hesitated a moment. "Thank you," he said softly.

Mr. Hanover gave him a wink and a reassuring nod. "I'll see you from the sidelines."

* * * *

The Muskie Festival parade had it all, Griffy marveled: marching bands, cheerleaders, and baton twirlers; fire, police, and sanitation departments; prizewinning horses, pigs, and sheep— all participated. But it was the National Freshwater Fishing Hall of Fame float the crowd had come to see.

Pike, Griffy, and Gil sat atop the float in *The Lucky 13* surrounded by iridescent, blue-green streamers that waved and glistened like lake water. The replica of their record-breaking catch hung behind them.

Andy Gibson, not one to miss a promotional opportunity, stood behind the fish yelling to the crowd like a sideshow peddler and throwing out cards inviting them to see the *real* record-breaking muskie—for a fee—now lying in state in the DNR's walk-in freezer.

"Seventy pounds! Two-inch, razor-sharp teeth! Prehistoric! Come see the beast!"

Spinner was not forgotten. The dog ran alongside the float barking and jumping up to catch the candy Pike, Griffy, and Gil threw out to the crowd.

"Sweet chedda cheese. It doesn't get any better than this." Pike smiled as he tossed out a handful of jawbreakers and gum.

Gil waved her best beauty queen wave and giggled.

Griffy held their double-eyed cane pole and cast it repeatedly toward the front of the float. He was trying really hard to enjoy his moment in the spotlight, but his thoughts kept drifting to his parents and to disappointment. He wished they could see him up here on top of this float. Lost in his thoughts, Griffy cast the pole again. Sudden movement on the parade route ahead, however, caught his eye and brought him back. A security guard was scuffling with some guy in the street. The man wouldn't step back to the curb. He was arguing with the guard and struggling to get around him.

"Hey, look." Pike poked Griffy. "We've got a stalker."

Griffy and Gil chuckled as their float glided slowly toward the scene. Griffy paused mid-cast and did a quick double take. *Wait a minute. That's no stalker.*

"That's my dad!" he cried out excitedly and stood up waving madly. "Dad! Dad!"

"Huh?" Pike asked, looking toward the man and then back to Griffy. "Hey, cool," he finally exclaimed. Then he and Gil stood and waved too.

Griffy's dad waved wildly back. "That's my son!" he yelled, pointing at Griffy.

The security guard reluctantly stepped aside. Griffy's dad ran up to the float and high-fived his son.

"No, it doesn't get any better this," Griffy beamed. "Sweet chedda cheese. It really, really doesn't."

See You Next Summer

It was the end of August and time for Griffy to head back to Chicago. He loaded his gear into Uncle Dell's SUV, looking very different than the boy who had arrived two months earlier. He was thinner, more muscular, and covered in scrapes and bruises. He also stood a little taller and walked with an air of confidence and determination. A thin scar running down his arm would stay with him for the rest of his life and serve as a reminder of his first great outdoor adventure: the day he fought a world record muskie and won.

Griffy sighed and adjusted his new camouflage baseball cap emblazoned with the insignia "Master Fisherman." Pike, wearing the same cap, limped over, careful not to put too much weight on his injured leg. The doctor just gave him permission to stop using crutches—after much pleading on Pike's part.

"Hey, I'm glad your dad came up," Pike said.

"Yeah, me too," Griffy replied, "even though it was only for a day. We had some fun together. It was good. And get this. He wants me to save my part of the prize money—all of it—for college. Yeah, right." Griffy pulled at the brim of his baseball cap. "I'm thinking new fishing gear and a lot of Tremblay's candy."

Pike laughed and nodded. "I hear ya. So, I'll see you next summer, right?"

"Oh, sure. I'll be here."

"Good," Pike grinned mischievously. "I've already started planning our next adventure." Pike's eyes sparkled in a way Griffy now knew meant trouble.

"Oh, no. Now what?" he asked with a nervous laugh.

"Next summer," Pike answered. Then he turned and started to hobble away.

"Come on," Griffy pleaded after him. "What? What is it?"

Pike turned back and shrugged innocently. "I'll see you next summer."

Be sure to check out *Ancient Elk Hunt* and *Snakehead Invasion*, the first and second books in the *Up North Adventure* series.

Two boys find themselves on a prehistoric quest, recovering fossils from the mysterious waters of Lost Land Lake. Are they ready to fight for justice?

When an exotic fish threatens to ruin Lost Land Lake, two boys become entangled in a treacherous mystery. Can they protect the lake they love?

www.facebook.com/upnorthadventure

Made in the USA
Middletown, DE
12 February 2020